UP IN FLAMES

HELLFIRE BOOK #6

ELLE JAMES

TWISTED PAGE INC

UP IN FLAMES

HELLFIRE BOOK #6

New York Times & USA Today
Bestselling Author

ELLE JAMES

This book is dedicated to my darling muse, Sweetpea. She gave us thirteen years of unconditional love and entertainment. That eight-pound ball of fluffy white frosting loved to eat everything she could get her mouth on and sleep curled up on the sofa. She'd take many tries before finally launching herself onto the lofty heights of the couch, but once there, she could spend hours sleeping. She reminded me of a salmon throwing herself upstream. No grace, just determination. I'll always remember her getting a running start to make it up the staircase and then sitting at the top, staring down at me. It was as if she was urging me to get on up there! I loved that little dog so much and will miss her forever. I hope she has all the treats she can eat, there, across the rainbow bridge. All my love to you, Sweetpea!

Escape with...

Elle James

aka Myla Jackson

AUTHOR'S NOTE

Enjoy these other books in the HELLFIRE Series
by Elle James

Hellfire Series
Hellfire, Texas (#1)
Justice Burning (#2)
Smoldering Desire (#3)
Hellfire in High Heels (#4)
Playing With Fire (#5)
Up in Flames (#6)
Total Meltdown (#7)

Visit ellejames.com for more titles and release dates
For hot cowboys, visit her alter ego Myla Jackson at
mylajackson.com
and join Elle James and Myla Jackson's Newsletter at
Newsletter

CHAPTER 1

"GET OUT." For the tenth time Kate practiced the words. This time, with even more emphasis than the last nine. "Get out!"

She pulled up to a stoplight and mashed the brakes. Kate hoped the police would get there before she did. Although she didn't like conflict, she'd gotten used to dealing with it on a daily basis in the Army. If it wasn't the hazard of being shot at, it was the unrest in the ranks. Soldiers away from home could get cranky and depressed, taking their stress out on each other.

Fortunately, the Army part of her life was over. If Bacchus hadn't developed a skittishness toward loud noises, they might have stayed in the service. However, due to his inability to handle the sound of gunfire and things that go bang, Bacchus had been retired. Kate, having met her enlistment obligation, had chosen to separate from the military and pursue adoption of the dog she'd trained, giving him a "forever home" with her.

"Get out!" she said again, getting used to the way the words rolled right off her tongue.

Bacchus whined and gave her a pathetic glance with his ears perked forward, as if he was trying, but couldn't quite understand why she'd want him to get out of the vehicle without her.

She patted the head of the Belgian Malinois sitting in the seat beside her. "It's okay," she said. "You don't have to get out. My ex does. You and I are going to be just fine," she told the dog.

Thankfully, the landlord was letting her out of her lease early. She had a new job in a new town, and she was going to start her life over now that she was out of the Army. She hadn't seen Randy in almost nine months, but even from a distance, he still had a way of twisting her words and making her feel like she was the one at fault when he'd been the one in the wrong all this time.

Her nine months of deployment to Afghanistan had left her feeling a little stronger and more confident in herself. This time when she asked him to leave—no, when she *told* him to leave—she wouldn't take him back. In fact, she was driving a truck pulling a rented trailer with every intention of moving all her stuff and starting over in another place.

She shot a glance at the dog in the passenger seat. "What do you think, Bacchus?"

His tongue hanging out, Bacchus turned to look at her as he panted. He gave a soft *woof.*

"I agree one hundred percent." She sighed. "It only took me nine months in the desert to figure it out."

She'd been back stateside for two weeks. During that time, she'd stayed in a hotel while she'd completed all of her out-processing to leave the Army. And she'd also taken care of the adoption of her dog Bacchus. She hadn't notified Randy that she'd returned from the desert, preferring to have everything in place when she did. She'd been offered a job in Hellfire, Texas. Her acceptance had been contingent on one thing and one thing only. She glanced again at Bacchus. "Just waiting for that call."

As if on cue, her phone rang through the speaker system of her vehicle. She hit the talk button when she recognized the phone number as the one from the sheriff's department in Hellfire. Her heart racing, she answered. "This is Kate."

"Kate, this is Sheriff Olson from Hellfire. You got a minute?"

Kate nodded though she knew he couldn't see her. "That's all I have, about one minute. I'm on my way to move my things from my apartment."

"It won't take long," the sheriff said. "I did some research. I think we can do what you asked."

A flash of joy and a healthy dose of hope burned

through Kate's chest. "That's good news. Then, Sheriff Olson, I accept."

"Great," Sheriff said. "When can I expect you to start?"

Kate chuckled. "How's Monday morning sound to you?"

"This Monday?" The sheriff asked with surprise in his tone.

"If you can get me started that soon I'd appreciate it," Kate said. "I just need to find a place to stay, and I'll be ready."

"I know someone who might have a garage apartment for rent—if you're interested."

"Oh, I'm interested," Kate said.

"How do you know? I haven't even told you anything about it."

Kate's lips thinned. "Does it have a roof?"

"Yes."

"Does it have an indoor shower?"

"Yes," the sheriff said. "In fact, it's fully furnished."

"Sold." Kate didn't care if it was painted purple with yellow polka dots. Anything would be better than what she was dealing with now. And anything was better than a tent in the desert or a Conex box converted into living quarters. Then she had a thought. "You say it's fully furnished?"

"Yes," the sheriff said. "The only drawback is the house next door burned down recently, and they're still cleaning up the debris. And construction will surely follow, so I'm sure you can get a good deal on renting the property. It'll be a great place just to start with, and then you can look for another as you get a feel for the town."

"Then I'll need somewhere to store a few of my things. I have a couple pieces of furniture and a few household items."

"We have a shed behind the sheriff's department. You can put your stuff out there for now if you want."

"Sounds perfect."

"If that doesn't work," the sheriff continued, "the nearest storage units are in Hole in The Wall, a town twenty miles west of Hellfire."

"Hole in The Wall?" Kate asked. "I've never heard of it." But then, she hadn't heard of Hellfire until she'd stumbled across the deputy sheriff advertisement.

The sheriff laughed. "You aren't used to small towns, are you?"

Kate snorted. "Not unless you consider San Antonio a small town."

"It can be pretty laid back here in Hellfire," the sheriff said. "Some would call it boring."

"I could use a little laid back and boring, right about now." Especially after what she would have to deal with in the next few minutes. She turned onto the street where her apartment complex was located. Her back stiffened, and her fingers tightened on the steering wheel. "Well, if that's all you need from me, I'll see you on Monday morning."

The moment of truth may have arrived, but the police had yet to show.

No matter. She'd get the party started without them. And if she had any problems, she'd just wait until they arrived and have them finish the job.

She pulled the truck towing the U-Haul trailer into the parking lot, made a wide turn and backed up toward the staircase that led to her second-floor apartment. It was early on a Friday afternoon. If Randy was holding a job, he might still be at work. That would give her time to load up as much of her crap as she could before he arrived home. If he wasn't working and he was home, then the fun would start earlier.

Kate got out of her truck and climbed the stairs to the second-story apartment. She slipped the key into the keyhole and turned the knob. The door pushed open easily.

The smell hit her first. That horrible rotten food, trash-that-hadn't-been-taken-out, and old-pizza-as-well-as-dirty-socks-and-clothing smell wafted into her nostrils and made her gag. The place in no way resembled the neatly cleaned apartment she'd left nine months ago. A pair of dirty jeans lay on the floor in the hallway with a belt still through the loops. A T-shirt lay slung across the top of the lampshade next to the couch. Old pizza boxes, dirty dishes, and sweaty drinking glasses sat making rings on her wooden coffee table.

Bacchus whined softly as he stood beside her.

The sounds of vehicles pulling up behind her made Kate turn. Two police vehicles pulled in and parked beside her U-Haul. Two officers emerged. She waved from the balcony and waited for them to join her at the door.

The first officer arrived. "Are you all right, ma'am?"

She nodded. "I'm fine."

"Is he here?" the second officer asked, his hand on his firearm.

Kate shook her head. "I don't know. This is as far as I've gotten. I was just opening the door and smelling the smell."

The officer grimaced. "Do you want us to go in first?"

"No, thanks. I'll go first." Kate entered, her heart sinking with every step. Any of the furniture remaining in the apartment would probably have to be tossed. In the hallway was the old secretary desk her grandmother had willed to her when she'd passed. Even that would need more work because of the damage from having wet drinking glasses laid on the top. The desk was one piece of furniture she could not get rid of. It was part of her family. The only piece that she had left, and the only connection that remained to the family she no longer had.

The damage to the rest of her furniture was worse than she'd first thought. The arm of the couch drooped down as if it had been broken. The television had a crack from one edge to the opposite corner as though it had been dropped. Kate glanced toward the kitchen where piles of dishes lay in the sink with mold growing on them.

As far as she was concerned, every bit of the dishes and utensils could be thrown in the trash. Other than a few items of clothing and her grandmother's desk, she really didn't care about anything else in the apartment. It was a good thing she'd called ahead and arranged for a local charity to come and collect everything she didn't want. They'd be there within two hours of her departure.

Pushing back her sleeves, she reached for the door to the bedroom and pushed it open.

Inside was just as much of a disaster as the rest of the apartment. It appeared as if the mattress box springs had given up the ghost and sagged in the middle, and there was a lump in the middle beneath the comforter.

Kate walked forward and pressed a hand to the lump.

A head popped up.

Kate let out a startled, "Eeep!"

A woman with bleached blond hair sat up, pulling a sheet over her naked breasts. "Who the hell are you?"

Anger bubbled up inside Kate. "I could ask the same."

The woman sneered. "I asked first."

Kate put her fists on her hips and stared at the woman in her bed. "Do you realize whose apartment you're in?"

"It's Randy's apartment." She glanced toward the bathroom door. "You better get out of here before I call the police."

A policeman stepped up behind Kate. "Need assistance?"

He had directed the question toward Kate, but the blonde in the bed answered. "Yes, officer, this woman is trespassing." She pointed at Kate. "Arrest her. Arrest her, now!"

The office shook his head. "Afraid not, ma'am. Miss Bradley's name is on the lease."

The blonde's brows screwed up, and she narrowed her eyes, staring at Kate. "You must be mistaken. This is Randy's apartment. He's lived here for as long as I've known him."

"And how long has that been?" Kate asked.

The woman pushed her hair back from her face with one hand. "At least eight or nine months."

Kate snorted. It hadn't taken Randy long to find someone else to warm his bed. And he hadn't even had the decency to break it off with her before he had. Instead, he'd taken advantage of her by living in her apartment rent-free, when he'd promised to pay the rent while she'd been gone.

A voice sounded from the bathroom. "Hey, sweetheart, do you know where I left m—" The door swung open, and Randy stood there with a towel loosely slung around his hips and his hair wet. His eyes widened, and his jaw dropped. "Kate, honey, when did you get back?"

"Not soon enough, it appears." Kate tilted her head toward the woman in the bed. "Get your girlfriend, and get out." There, it hadn't been nearly as hard as she'd thought. And the sense of satisfaction was worth the effort.

"Kate, it's not what it looks like." Randy grabbed a wadded-up T-shirt from the top of the dresser and pulled it over his head.

"And what does it look like?" Kate asked.

"Well, you know..." He shrugged, grimaced and held open his arms. "I missed you. Don't I get a hug?"

The thought of touching the man who'd been sleeping with another woman while she, Kate, had been out defending their country, nearly made her want to puke. She shook her head. "Nope. Get your girlfriend and get out."

"You can't mean that," Randy said.

Kate jerked her head toward the officers behind her. "I mean it. And I brought back up just to make sure it happens."

Randy frowned. "You can't kick me out. You sublet this apartment to me."

Kate raised her eyebrows in challenge. "You have paperwork to prove it?"

"No, it was a verbal agreement."

She lifted her chin. "Do you have any cancelled checks as proof that you paid rent?"

Randy's eyes narrowed.

Kate laughed. "You don't because you didn't." One side of Kate's mouth pulled up in a smirk. "Right. Not one dime. After the first month's rent was behind, the landlord contacted me. I have been paying the rent the entire time I was gone. Which makes this my apartment and makes you a squatter."

Randy's eyes widened as he spotted the policemen behind Kate. "Really? You brought the police?"

"I had to," Kate said. "I wrote you several times asking you to move out."

His eyes narrowed. "No, you didn't."

Kate's jaw tightened. "I did, and you signed for the letters." She pulled the stack of certified receipts from her back pocket and held them in front of him. "I have proof. So, I repeat: *Get. Out.*"

Randy's gaze shot left then right. "You can't do this to me. You need to give me some time."

"I gave you nine months." Kate jerked her thumb over her shoulder. "Time's up."

Randy looked down at his legs below the towel

wrapped around his waist. "You could at least give me time to get dressed."

She didn't care if he had to walk out naked. The man had to go. "I gave you nine months to get your life in order. That's all I'm giving you."

"I don't remember you being such a bitch." Randy glared at her. "We used to be good together."

"In your mind," Kate said. "You always managed to manipulate me and make me feel like it was my fault things weren't working out."

He grabbed a pair of jeans from the floor. "I can't help it that you were wishy-washy."

"Well, I'm not now." She stepped back and angled her head toward the policemen. "This man is trespassing in my apartment."

The officers nodded. "Sir, if you two would get dressed, we'll escort you and your companion out."

The bleached blonde scooted to the side of the bed, wrapping the sheet around her naked body. She glared at Randy. "You mean to tell me this isn't your apartment?"

He shoved a hand through his hair. "Oh, shut up and get dressed."

She tossed her hair and snorted like a horse. Then she grabbed clothes from the floor and hurried toward the bathroom.

"At least let me get my jeans and shoes on," Randy said.

Kate shrugged. "Fine. But make it fast."

12

"What about my things?" he asked.

"The apartment is mine. Everything in it is mine. You're lucky I'm letting you take the jeans. Now, could you hurry it up? I'll throw whatever I don't want out. You can sift through it when I'm done."

"Really, Kate, be reasonable. There are things..." He took a step toward her.

Bacchus growled, baring his teeth.

Kate patted the dog's head. "You're done here. Just leave."

Jeans in hand, Randy turned away and dropped his towel. As he pulled the jeans up over his naked ass, a bag fell from the back pocket of his pants.

Kate stiffened. "Uh, Randy, you dropped something." She moved aside to make sure the policemen could see what he'd dropped.

Randy turned and looked at what was on the floor. His face blanched.

When he bent to grab the packet, a policeman stepped forward. "Sir, I'm going to have to ask you to step away."

"Fuck." Randy hesitated, but then thought better of it and stepped backward.

The policeman drew the gun from his holster and aimed it at Randy. "Sir, put your hands behind your head and turn around."

With two cops blocking his route of escape, Randy had no other choice but to do as he was told. He locked his hands behind his head and turned.

While one cop held the gun on Randy, the other cop bent to retrieve a plastic baggie full of what looked like white powder.

"Is that what I think that is?" Kate asked, holding her hands up as if afraid to touch anything.

"If it's what I think it is," the cop said, "it's cocaine."

Kate shuddered. "I don't know what I ever saw in you, Randy."

The blonde chose that moment to open the bathroom door. She took one look at the cop holding the gun and screamed, "Oh my God! Oh my God! Don't shoot."

For the next few minutes the policemen frisked Randy and his girlfriend. They handcuffed their wrists together and led them out of the building and down the stairs to the squad cars. More cops appeared and combed through her apartment, looking for additional drugs. By the time they'd finished it was dark outside, and Kate was allowed to begin moving the things she was going to keep.

The police helped her move her grandmother's desk into the trailer before they left. Once she was alone, Kate packed a few of her clothing items into a suitcase and a couple of photo albums of her family. A final trip back inside, and she was done.

The charity she'd called arrived with their van.

Kate stood in the doorway of the apartment she'd shared with Randy for a year prior to her deployment. At twenty-nine years old, she'd thought that she would have accumulated more items that she might have cared about.

Apparently not.

It was time for her to start over.

She held the door for Bacchus. He leaped up into the passenger seat of her pickup. Kate slid in behind the wheel, and the two of them headed north.

A job and a new life awaited Kate in Hellfire, Texas. She was determined not to make the same mistakes she'd made with Randy. As she shifted into gear, she vowed that men would remain off limits. At least for the near future. They were nothing but trouble, and she had a track record of picking losers.

CHAPTER 2

CHANCE GRAYSON REVVED the engine of his dirt bike as he paused at the top of the embankment. He glanced down at the narrow, winding trail leading to the bottom of a ravine and ultimately out onto the highway. Rocky, full of bumps and dangerous, it was just the kind of track he found most challenging. He didn't pause for long before he tipped the front wheel over the edge and plummeted down the hillside.

The faster he went and the more challenging the course, the less time he had to remember.

The handlebar jerked in his grip as he twisted it back and forth, following the narrow path through the bramble, brush and trees. On more than one occasion, he'd thought about letting go of the handlebar and seeing where the bike and the terrain would take him. If he hit a tree head-on, the helmet he wore would do little to protect the rest of his body. He'd either die or break every bone in his body. So far, the subconscious desire to live overruled those self-destructive thoughts and made him focus on traversing the path all the way to the bottom and the smooth pavement of the highway leading into Hellfire.

Now traveling along fairly even asphalt, he had little to task his mind. The road was straight, leaving too much time for his memories to resurface and haunt him.

Chance twisted the throttle, giving the bike all the fuel it could take, shooting it forward, faster and faster. He shot past one hundred miles per hour as he reached the outer edges of Hellfire.

Nash would bust his ass if he caught him going that fast. He wouldn't hear the end of it from all his brothers, his sister and parents. He throttled back and let the motorcycle slow on its own, dropping back to eighty, then seventy, sixty and ultimately a tame forty as he passed the first houses on Main Street. A truck with a moving trailer blocked the road as it backed into a driveway.

Chance came to a complete stop, frowning. The driveway belonged to Lola Engel. The fact that a strange truck was backing in wasn't what had his brow dipping. Lola's house had burned to the ground in a fire a couple weeks ago. She was lucky to be alive. The charred debris had yet to be completely cleared, making it a sad reminder of what a fire can do to an old, wood-framed building.

Though the fire had destroyed the house, the detached garage still stood. The side closest to the house had been covered in soot. Hell, Chance had been there to help douse the flames and keep the fire from spreading to nearby structures.

As close as the garage was, it had to still smell of smoke. It was hard to get that smell out after a fire. Someone would have to be pretty desperate to rent the apartment above.

Because the road was blocked, Chance had to remained stopped, his foot on the ground, balancing the bike between his thighs.

The truck continued expertly backward, pushing the trailer straight onto the concrete drive. Not every man had the knack for backing a trailer. The windows were tinted, so Chance couldn't see the man driving. But he had respect for his skills moving it up the narrow drive.

Curiosity made him pull to the side of the road and engage the kickstand. He wasn't expected at the fire station until the next day. His workout could wait. He wanted to know who was moving into his town. Perhaps he could offer to help the guy.

Then the "guy" switched off the engine, shoved the driver's door open and dropped down from the pickup. Only it wasn't a guy. She was a tall, slim drink of water with rich brown hair and deep green eyes. Without looking his direction, she rounded the front of the pickup and opened the passenger side. A large, light-brown dog leaped out of the seat and ran toward Chance.

Bracing himself, Chance stood fast, praying the dog was friendly and only wanted him to scratch his belly.

The dog sniffed his pant leg and circled him before jumping up on his hind legs and planting his forepaws on Chance's chest.

Chance staggered backward, and normally he wouldn't have fallen, but his heels hit the curb. He stumbled and fell on his ass.

"Bacchus. *Platz!*" The woman with the dark brown hair raced toward them.

The dog backed away and dropped to his belly, still watching Chance, his head canted to one side.

"I'm sorry." The brunette placed a hand on the dog's collar. "He's never done that before." She frowned down at the animal, though her hand gently rubbed the dog's neck.

Chance picked himself up from the ground and dusted off his jeans. "It's okay. I think he likes me."

"Some police dog you are," she muttered and stuck out her hand. "I'm Kate Bradley."

Chance gripped her hand in his, a spark of aware-ness rippling up his arm and through his body. His brow dipped. He hadn't felt anything like that in couple of years. And he wasn't sure he liked it.

Pushing aside the feeling, he shook her hand and pasted a smile on his face. "Chance Grayson." He tipped his head toward the garage. "New in town?"

She nodded. "I am. Just getting settled in."

"Need a hand moving anything?"

"Not in here. I was told it was fully furnished."

Tipping his head toward the charred remains of Lola's house, Chance grimaced. "Hopefully the apartment doesn't smell like smoke."

"Frankly I don't care what it smells like. I just need a place to sleep and shower." She glanced toward the staircase leading up to the apartment over the garage. "If you'll excuse me, I need to get moving. I start work tomorrow, and I want to be ready."

"Work?" Chance cocked his eyebrows.

Kate turned away from him and opened the back of the trailer. From inside, she grabbed an army-green duffel bag and a small suitcase. Slinging the duffel over her shoulder, she started for the stairs. "I've got a job as a deputy with the sheriff's department. Bacchus and I are a package deal."

"That's right. Nash was telling me they had a new deputy. I don't remember him saying anything about a police dog."

She paused, glancing over her shoulder. "Nash?"

Chance tipped his head toward other suitcases in the back of the nearly empty trailer. Only one item of furniture stood strapped to the interior. "Taking all of this up?"

She shook her head. "Only the suitcases and bags. The desk is going into storage."

He shoved a bag under his arm, curled his fingers around two suitcase handles and followed the woman up the stairs. "Nash is my brother. He's a deputy. He mentioned a new recruit would be starting. I didn't realize it would be so soon."

"Yeah, I freed up sooner than I expected," Kate said, her tone flat, her back stiff. She stopped at the top of the stairs and dropped the bags she'd carried. Reaching over the top of the door, she ran her hand along the door frame. "Ms. Engel said the key would be up here somewhere. Ah, there it is." With the key in hand, she unlocked the door and threw it open. "Is it safe to leave keys out where anyone can get to them?"

"It's a small town," Chance said. "Most people don't even lock their front doors at night."

"In this day and age?" She shook her head. "Crime doesn't skip the small towns."

"No, it doesn't." Chance's glance shot to the rubble next to the garage.

Kate moved the duffel bag and the suitcase through the door and stepped aside for Chance to enter. "What happened to the house?"

"Some crazy son of a bitch tried to burn it down, with Lola inside."

Kate's eyebrow lifted. "Seriously? I spoke to Ms. Engel. She's okay, right?"

"My coworker, Daniel, got her out in time."

"Your coworker?"

"A fellow firefighter from the Hellfire station."

She cocked an eyebrow. "Oh, so you're a fire-fighter?"

He nodded. "One of the few full-timers. Most of the department is made up of volunteers."

"Good to know, in case I set the kitchenette on fire." Her lips twisted into a grimace. "I'm a terrible cook."

"Not to worry. There's a great diner a couple blocks down. They serve food like your mother cooked."

Kate shook her head. "My mother worked a full-time job. She was a terrible cook as well. I think it's genetic." She reached for one of the suitcases Chance carried. When their hands touched, she frowned and jerked her hand away. Grabbing it with her other hand, she tipped her head toward the middle of the small room. "You can set those anywhere. I'll sort through them later. I need to get to the sheriff's department to unload the desk. I want to turn in the rented trailer this afternoon."

After Chance set the cases and the bag on the floor, he straightened. "Is that all you have?"

"When I found out the apartment was furnished, I donated the rest of my household goods to charity." Kate's jaw tightened. "None of it was worth keeping."

He'd bet there was a story behind the hard look.

An ex-boyfriend who'd done her wrong? The bastard.

His fists curled.

Based on the dark circles beneath her eyes, she probably hadn't slept much since whatever breakup she'd had to endure.

Not that he cared. Chance wasn't a candidate for picking up the pieces of someone else's life. He couldn't even pick up his own since leaving the military. "If you want to follow me, I'll show you where the sheriff's department is."

"Thanks." She followed him out of the apartment, locking the door behind her.

He mounted his dirt bike and waited as Kate and Bacchus climbed into the truck.

The brake lights blinked, and the truck's engine roared to life.

Chance drove his bike past the hood of the truck, aiming for the sheriff's department, located a block from the fire station. He told himself Kate was just another face in town. The electric currents he'd felt when their hands had touched had been purely imaginary. He wasn't in the market for a relationship, and she probably wasn't either. Which was just as well.

Once he'd done his civic duty to welcome the new deputy to town, Chance would head to the fire station and work out on the weights. Riding a dirt bike was strenuous, but he still had memories pushing at the back of his mind. Pumping iron and a long jog helped increase his endorphins and wear him out so that he could get a little sleep between nightmares.

Being home for an entire year since he'd left the military, he'd thought he'd be past the bad dreams. But they still plagued him every night as he lay his head on a pillow and closed his eyes.

As soon as he drifted off, he was back in Afghanistan and the day his heart shattered into a million pieces. He relived those last few minutes of Sandy's life as she bled out in his arms.

A MAN who looked much like Chance Grayson stepped out of the sheriff's office as Kate pulled her truck and trailer into the parking lot. He frowned as the man on the motorcycle slid up next to him.

Kate lowered her window and caught a few of the words they exchanged.

"Found her unloading at Lola's," Chance was saying. He turned to Kate. "Kate, Nash Grayson. Nash, Kate Bradley." He touched two fingers to his temple toward her and faced his brother. "She's all yours."

"See you at dinner tonight?" Nash asked.

Chance shrugged. "Maybe."

Nash's brow dipped. "Maybe we'll save you a seat at the table. Mom and Dad got back in town last night. They'll want to see your ugly mug."

Chance's lip curled in a grimace. "Sorry. Yes, I'll be there."

Another glance her way and a slight tip of his head and Chance Grayson shot forward, burning rubber on the pavement."

"Damn it!" Nash shook his head. "I need to impound that motorcycle. It's barely street legal."

Kate climbed down from the truck, snapped a lead on Bacchus and let him jump down beside her.

Nash Grayson waited on the sidewalk for her to join him. "Welcome to Hellfire." He held out his hand.

Kate shook it, not feeling the same electric charge she'd experienced at Chance's touch. Perhaps the ground near Lola's garage apartment was somehow charged with electricity. That could be the only explanation for the jolt she'd felt. After kicking her ex-boyfriend out of her apartment back in San Antonio, she sure as hell wasn't interested in starting anything new. Men were trouble and strictly off limits. She needed to get her life together before she even considered dating again. If that took two, three or more years, she didn't mind. That's what BOB was for. Her battery-operated boyfriend had kept her company on more than one occasion, and it wasn't nearly as messy physically or emotionally.

The thought of BOB, Chance and the need to satisfy herself seemed incongruous the moment she shook Nash Grayson's hand. Kate released her grip and jammed her hands into her jean's pockets. "Is Sheriff Olson in?"

"Kate Bradley?" A booming voice called out.

"Yes, sir." Kate looked over Nash's shoulder at a tall, barrel-chested man, with salt-and-pepper gray hair and bright blue eyes. He grinned and closed the distance between them.

She held out her hand. "I got here as soon as I could."

He gripped her hand in a strong but gentle hold. "You don't have to start work Monday, if you aren't ready. I'm sure you have business to take care of with your move."

She smiled. "I appreciate the extra time, but I don't need it." What she really needed was to get to work. The sooner, the better. During her deployment, they hadn't had days off. She was used to working every day without a break. Work helped keep her too busy to think about her failed relationship with Randy and the fact she had nothing to show for being almost thirty years old. No one waiting for her with open arms...hell, no home and no stuff to call her own.

She would miss being a part of the Army. During deployment, her unit had become her surrogate family. Now that they were back, the soldiers had gone home to their loved ones, leaving Kate to go home to a cheating boyfriend and a trashed apartment.

She had no one to blame but herself. Unlike many of the soldiers in her unit, she'd looked forward to going to Afghanistan. The time overseas had given her an excuse to put off the decision she'd known she needed to make about Randy. Kicking someone out of your apartment wasn't easy when things weren't rocky, but surprisingly easy when she'd returned, and he'd been in bed with another woman. She should thank Randy for making the decision for her.

"Have it your way. We can get started training you and your dog on how things work around Hellfire."

"Great. We're ready." She glanced down at her partner. "This is Bacchus. He's smart, healthy and has a lot of good years left in him."

"Why did they retire him?" the sheriff asked.

She scratched behind Bacchus's ears. "After a particularly close explosion, he developed a nervousness for loud noises. It affected his ability to focus on bomb sniffing. He has a good nose. All we need to give him is something non-explosive to sniff for.

"I have some marijuana and cocaine we can use for training purposes. It's controlled. You'll have to check it in and out whenever you want to work with it."

Kate nodded. "Good. We'll start tomorrow training for drugs."

"I have uniforms on order. We didn't have any in your size. They should be here in three days. In the meantime, you can report to work in jeans and a department T-shirt. If you'll come inside, I'll get a couple for you."

"Yes, sir." Kate popped a salute before she remembered she didn't have to anymore.

Sheriff Olson and Nash Grayson chuckled.

Her cheeks heating, Kate squared her shoulders and gave a smiling grimace. "Old habits die hard."

"Don't worry about it." The sheriff led the way into the office.

Kate and Bacchus fell in step behind him.

Sheriff Olson turned to Kate. "I'll be right back." He disappeared through a door into what appeared to be a storeroom.

Grayson stepped up beside Kate. "You were in the Army?"

"Yes, sir," Kate responded.

"Chance spent ten years on active duty," Nash said. "You two probably have a lot in common."

Kate turned to face the deputy. "Chance? Your brother on the motorcycle?"

Nash's brow wrinkled. "That's right, you two met. He led you here."

"Yeah, we met, all right." And touched and felt something that couldn't be there. Kate reminded herself she'd sworn off men. Especially ones who had trouble written all over them. And Chance seemed to fit into that category.

Sheriff Olson emerged from the storeroom carrying a couple of shirts. He handed them to Kate.

"These might be a little large on you, but they're the smallest size we have. You're the first female we've had in the department in a long time." The sheriff scratched his head. "Hell, you might be the first female deputy we've ever had in this county. I don't know why we let that happen."

"Probably because no females have responded to your ads," Nash pointed out.

The sheriff's lips twisted. "That's right. And certainly, none who had the qualifications. Your background on the military police force made you an ideal candidate."

"I'm glad all my military training and experience will come in handy," Kate said.

"It will," the sheriff assured her. "We've scheduled you for the training academy the month after next to learn all the ins and outs of civilian law in Texas. This week we'll get you certified to drive our service vehicles, take you to the range to qualify with your weapon, and then we'll pair you with another deputy for your first week of on the job training." The sheriff clapped his hands. "Sound like a plan?"

"Yes, sir." She held one of the shirts up in front of her. It was large and would probably hang down to the middle of her thighs. But she could tuck the hem into her jeans and make it work. "Is that all for now?"

The sheriff nodded. "We'll bring you on board tomorrow with computer access and set up your login and passwords for reporting. For now, you might as well get all settled in and rested up. You have a busy week ahead."

Kate smiled. "Good. I like it that way." The busier she was, the sooner she'd learn all she needed to know to be a good deputy for the department. She tensed. "One other thing..."

"What's that?" Sheriff Olson raised an eyebrow.

"Bacchus," Kate said. "He'll be with me through all the training?" She held her breath, afraid the sheriff had changed his mind.

The sheriff nodded. "As agreed. And his training will begin tomorrow as well. As we don't have any other members on the force familiar with dog training, you'll be completely in charge of how it'll be done. You'll have access to what you need for training props, and you'll have time during the day to work with him. My only concern is taking him to the firing range."

"I thought about that. I want him to be exposed to gunfire as much as I can. I want him to learn not to be afraid of it."

"Good. And how is he for attacking bad guys?"

"He was trained early on in his career to attack on command, but he's a little rusty. His primary responsibility for the past few years has been to sniff out bombs." She patted Bacchus's head and met the sheriff's gaze. "He's good. Just needs a refresher."

"Again, I'll leave it to you."

A woman appeared in a doorway. "Sheriff, Joe Dietrich for you on line one."

The sheriff gave Kate a wry smile. "Duty calls, even on my day off. See you tomorrow morning."

"Yes, sir," Kate snapped her heels together and waited for the sheriff to leave the room before she relaxed. She glanced toward Nash.

The man had a grin on his face.

Kate frowned. "What?"

He shook his head. "Nothing."

"I know," she said. "I have to remember I'm not in the military anymore."

"I didn't say that." Nash grinned.

Kate sighed. "You didn't have to."

"I understand the sheriff is going to let you store some of your stuff in the shed out behind the office. Let's take care of that, so you can turn in your trailer."

"Thanks." Kate followed Nash out of the office.

"If you'll drive around back, I'll unlock the shed."

Kate held the door for Bacchus and climbed into the truck beside him. A few moments later, she pulled around to the back of the office and stopped in front of the shed Nash stood beside.

Between the two of them, they moved the desk into the shed along with a box of memorabilia Kate had salvaged from her apartment. She wouldn't need it anytime soon. When she found a home of her own, she'd get it out and look through it. Until then, she had work to get trained up for what they needed her to do.

The sun was heading for the horizon by the time Kate climbed into her truck beside Bacchus.

Nash leaned close to the open window. "Look, it's Sunday evening, you're new in town and probably haven't had a chance to stock your refrigerator. Why don't you come out to the ranch for dinner tonight?"

"I hate to impose," Kate said, but her stomach rumbled, reminding her she hadn't had anything to eat the entire day.

"You won't be imposing. The ladies will be excited to have another female at the table and you can get to know some of the residents of Hellfire."

"I don't know…" Kate hesitated, her gaze going to the dog on the seat beside her.

Nash tilted his head and cocked an eyebrow. "We can probably rustle up some chow for Bacchus as well."

Her stomach rumbled again. This time loud enough Nash heard.

He laughed. "You might as well say yes."

Bacchus woofed softly.

Kate grinned. "I feel like I'm being overruled by my stomach and my dog. I am hungry, but…I really shouldn't."

He scribbled the address on a sheet of paper from his notepad and handed it to her. "We eat in an hour. That should give you plenty of time to turn in your trailer and make a run back to Lola's garage, if you need to, before heading out to the ranch."

Kate glanced down at the piece of paper. Her eyes flooded, and her throat tightened. "Thank you," she whispered. She blinked back the moisture and pasted a grin on her face before lifting her head. "But I can't. I have too much to do to get ready for my first day on the job. And Bacchus has never been on a ranch." She didn't have that much to do. But she just wasn't up to being the odd duck at a family gathering.

He grinned. "Bacchus will be fine. And if you change your mind or get finished early, you're still welcome to come. I hope to see you there." Nash stepped away from the truck and waved as Kate drove past him.

Her new life was just beginning, and already she'd been invited to share a meal with some of the residents of her new hometown.

She prayed she wasn't reading too much into her initial impression of Hellfire. She might be wrong, but it sure felt like home.

Things were looking up. She'd shed a bad boyfriend, started a new career and had her dog beside her. Yes, things were definitely looking up.

Kate looked around, her eyes narrowing as she took in the quiet beauty of Hellfire's Main Street.

What could possibly go wrong?

She headed back to her apartment, pulled into the driveway and stared up at the stairs leading to her new home. The refrigerator was empty, no one was waiting there to welcome her, and she'd had a perfectly good invitation to dinner. Why the hell had she declined?

Kate glanced down at the address Nash had given her. She punched it into the map application on her cell phone. It was only a few miles out of town. Though she'd grown up in Texas, she'd lived in the city and had never been on a real Texas ranch. What was stopping her?

She glanced across the cab at Bacchus. "Wanna go to a ranch for dinner?"

Bacchus stoic non-reply was enough for Kate. She didn't want to be alone her first night in town, and she was hungry.

CHAPTER 3

SUNDAY NIGHT DINNER should have been a place to come to relax with family and unwind. Lately, Chance would have preferred to skip it altogether. His well-meaning siblings had gotten it into their heads that he needed help. If his parents hadn't just returned from one of their many traveling adventures, he might have called and said he wasn't feeling well and wanted to hit the sack early to be ready for work the next day.

They'd know immediately he was faking it, but he didn't care. He didn't feel like putting up with Nash's digs and Becket's attempts at psychoanalyzing him in his cowboy kind of way. Just because Nash, Becket and Rider all had women in their lives now didn't mean Chance had to hook up with some female to be whole. He almost turned his bike around and drove away. But he didn't.

If he didn't show up, his mother would be unhappy. And when Ann Grayson was unhappy, Big John Grayson let his entire family know. Happy wife…happy life. *Make mama happy. Now!*

He pulled up to the ranch house and parked his motorcycle on the grass. Chance squared his shoulders, climbed the porch steps and entered through the front door.

Following the sound of voices, he made his way to the back of the house, in the direction of the kitchen.

There, he found his mother, Becket's black-haired, blue-eyed woman, Kinsey, Nash's red-haired sweetheart, Phoebe, and his sister Lily.

"Chance, honey." His mother engulfed him in a hug so tight he could barely catch his breath. "I'm so glad you decided to be here for dinner."

"I live here, Mother. Why wouldn't I?" He kissed the top of her faded auburn hair.

"Lily tells me that you've missed more Sunday dinners than you make. Why is that?" His mother stared up at him, a worried frown puckering her brow.

Chance shot a glare at Lily. "I've been busy."

"Too busy for family?"

"Sometimes," he hedged. Definitely too busy for family interference in his life.

"Well, now that we're home, you'll have to make time for family." His mother lifted her chin and gave him a hard stare. "We've always had family dinner on

Sunday night, even after you boys grew up. You missed too many while deployed. I expect you to make them up and then some." She stared at him for a long moment, her face hard, determined. Then she relaxed and smiled. "Besides, I love seeing your handsome face at the dinner table. You wouldn't deprive me of seeing my son, would you?"

His cheeks burned at the not-so-subtle admonishment. "Mom, sometimes I work on Sunday nights."

"Those I'll excuse. Any other time, you'd have to be sick or dying to miss. In which case, we'll bring dinner to you." She patted her hand against his chest. "Understood?"

He captured her hand in his and smiled. "You drive a hard bargain, Mrs. Grayson." He kissed her cheek. "I'll do my best to be here."

Her smile lit the room. "That's my boy." She turned to the counter and dug a large wooden spoon into a bowl of potato salad. "Now, we only have to work on finding you a partner to share life with."

"Whoa, wait a minute." Chance held up both hands. "I don't need you to find me a partner. I'm a die-hard bachelor. I don't need a woman in my life."

"Pooh." His mother waved her hand over her shoulder. "You don't even know what you don't know. A woman will make your life complete. And children are the happy icing on the cake."

Lily choked back laughter. "Chance, you should see your face." She doubled over, laughing.

Chance glared at her and frowned at his mother's back. "Mom. Please. Can you leave me to my own life?"

She smiled over her shoulder. "Of course, dear. Love is a delicate matter that has a way of finding you when you least expect it. It'll happen for you." Then she muttered beneath her breath.

Chance could swear she said, "With a little help."

"No, ma'am. I'm not interested in dating anyone here in Hellfire."

"Then we can go to Hole in the Wall." She looked up and grinned. "Have you been to the Ugly Stick Saloon lately? That Audrey Anderson hires some pretty young ladies to help run the place. Maybe you can find someone there."

"Mom, I don't want to find someone. I'm happy the way I am."

"Oh, sweetie." She shook her head. "You don't know what you're talking about. Trust me. You're not happy the way you are. You're miserable and lonely. You need someone else in your life."

Chance shook his head. He wasn't going to convince his mother otherwise. "Where's Dad?"

"Out back with your brothers. They should have the grill going by now. We're having steak and chicken."

"Mom," Nash poked his head in the door of the

kitchen. "Did I mention, I invited the new deputy to dinner?"

"No, you didn't." Mrs. Grayson frowned for a second and then smiled. "But we'll have plenty of food for one more. When will he be here?"

"*She* just pulled into the driveway," Nash said.

"You invited Kate?" Chance asked.

"I did. I figured she'd be hungry and have nothing in her pantry. Plus, she would probably like to meet some of the county residents." He reached out and grabbed Phoebe's hand. "Come on. I want you to meet Kate."

Chance's groin tightened at the thought of the dark-haired deputy. He shouldn't be feeling that way. Guilt roiled in his belly.

"Have you met the new lady deputy, Chance?" his mother asked.

His jaw tightened. "I have."

"Really?" She raised an eyebrow. "And what did you think of her?"

"Hopefully, she'll be an asset to the sheriff's department." He flung a hand to the side. "What am I supposed to think about her?"

"Is she pretty? Is she nice?" His mother wiped her hands on a towel. "I suppose I'll have to see for myself." She followed Phoebe and Nash.

Lily's mouth twisted into a knowing smirk. "She's pretty, isn't she?"

Chance shrugged. "If you're into that kind of

look."

"And what kind of look is that?"

Badass, tough, beautiful. He bit his tongue to keep from saying any of that. "You'll have to judge for yourself. I'm going to help with the grilling." He beat a hasty retreat to the back porch where he found Rider, Becket and his father.

"Where'd Nash go?" Big John Grayson held a long spatula in his hand. "I thought he was bringing the steaks."

"You'll have to wait." Chance's jaw hardened. "He and Phoebe went out front to greet our guest."

"Guest?" Rider's eyes widened. "I didn't know we were having guests."

"Guest. Only one."

"Oh, yeah?" Becket turned toward the house. "Who?"

"The new deputy. Apparently, Nash invited her."

Becket grinned. "Good. I wanted to meet her. Nash has had nothing but good things to say about her. Did you know she was in the Army?"

Chance frowned. "No." That would explain why she held herself with a military bearing he didn't see outside the armed forces.

"She was a member of the military police and trained with the military war dogs. Her one condition for hiring on with the sheriff's department was that she came with her MWD." Becket shook his head. "I was surprised to hear Sheriff Olson agreed."

"Hell, who wouldn't? Those military dogs are highly trainable." Big John frowned. "But that's not getting the steaks cooked." He headed for the house.

"Stay, Dad." Chance held up his hand. "I'll get the steaks." He'd just turned to re-enter the house when his sister Lily appeared in the doorway carrying a tray of raw steaks.

"Looking for these?" she asked with a smile.

"Yes." Chance took the tray from her and carried it to his waiting father.

"Will there be room for some chicken?" his mother said, carrying another tray with several chicken breasts.

"I'll make room," Big John said. "Anything for my baby." He winked at his wife, took the tray from her and set it down beside the steaks. Then he turned and swept Ann into his arms. "It's good to be home and surrounded by family." He gave her a big smack on her lips and grinned. "Although I love getting away with my bride."

"Stop, John." Ann batted at John's chest, her cheeks flushing a rosy red. "The children."

He laughed. "They aren't children anymore." He looked around at his sons and daughter. "I believe they know how they got here." He winked at Chance and kissed his wife again.

Ann wrapped her arms around her husband's neck and returned the kiss. When he set her back on her feet, she chuckled. "I do believe you make a good

41

point. However, if they know where they came from, what's taking them so long to grace us with grandchildren? I might be convinced to slow my travels if I had a few grandchildren around to spoil." She raised both eyebrows and gave Becket, Rider, Chance and Lily all a pointed look.

Becket reached out a hand to Kinsey as she stepped down from the porch. "I guess it's not too soon to share our news."

Kinsey blushed and looked around. "I thought you were going to wait to announce it when everyone was here."

Becket tipped his head toward the back door where Nash had just stepped out and held the door for Phoebe and the new deputy. "Everyone's here now."

"Okay then," Kinsey laughed. "I guess it's okay."

"I asked Kinsey to marry me," Becket said.

Kinsey's cheeks flushed a bright pink, and she grinned. "And I said yes."

"We're getting married!" Becket shouted, hugged Kinsey and spun her in a circle. Then he set her on her feet and kissed her soundly.

The family gathered around, congratulating the happy couple.

When Chance could get close enough to give his brother a hug, he chuckled. "Thanks for taking the pressure off the rest of us. I hope this means you'll be delivering on the grandchildren soon, as well."

Kinsey slipped her arm through Becket's. "We want four. Two boys and two girls."

"Good. That ought to hold off the grandparents."

"Don't think you're off the hook, Chance Grayson," his mother said from behind him. "I want all my children to be happily married. And I expect grandchildren from all of them."

"Damn," Chance muttered. "When did she sneak up behind me?"

Becket laughed. "About the time you were thanking me for taking the pressure off you. Don't worry. She'll have a bevy of ladies lined up for you to choose from."

"That's what I'm afraid of. Not all of us are the marrying kind."

"Chance, don't think you're immune to love. Give it time," his mother said. "There's someone for everyone. You just have to be open to the possibilities."

Chance's chest ached, and his throat tightened. Surrounded by his family, he suddenly felt as if he couldn't get enough air in his lungs. While everyone was congratulating Becket, Chance slipped away to the barn, hoping no one would notice his absence. He wanted to jump on his bike and drive away. Only speed and the wind in his face helped him to forget what he'd had and what he'd lost in the split second it took for the bullet to pierce her heart. He entered the shadowy darkness of the barn.

His mother had said there was someone out there

for everyone. Chance had found that someone in Army Specialist Sandy Meyers. He'd met her on his last tour to Afghanistan and had immediately fallen in love with the beautiful, sandy-haired blonde. She'd made him laugh when he'd thought he'd forgotten how. She'd shown him the light in the darkness of war and made him dream of a future he never thought possible.

He'd thought the few stolen kisses they'd managed to sneak would be the precursor to making love for the first time when they returned stateside. But one day when they'd been jogging inside the wire around the perimeter of camp, a Taliban rebel had fired a shot, aiming at Chance. He'd missed his target and hit Sandy instead. She'd bled out before Chance could get her back to the camp hospital. The field surgeon on duty had told him they couldn't have saved her, even if he'd gotten her back sooner. The bullet ripped through her heart, killing her in seconds.

He remembered trying to carry her back, while trying to hold a hand against the wound in her chest, praying as he ran that it wasn't too late. She'd been dead before he'd reached the hospital, her head lolling, her arms and legs flopping with every step he took. But Chance held out hope that the medical staff could bring her back to life. He'd yelled at them to use the paddles, perform CPR, do something. Anything. But don't let her die.

As he'd stood in front of a stall, the memories washed over him like a tsunami, pushing at the walls he'd tried to erect around his heart and mind. The bullet had been meant for him. Intel had learned that the Taliban had sent their sniper to take out the Army Ranger who'd killed one of their revered leaders. He'd then worn a vest filled with explosives into a crowded market. Before he'd detonated himself, he'd shouted that he was there in retribution for the murder of their leader and to blame the Americans for the destruction he'd unleashed that day.

Twenty-seven civilians had died in that market, seven of whom were small children.

By that evening, Chance had lost the woman he'd hoped to spend his life with, and he'd been blamed for the deaths of twenty-seven Afghan civilians.

Anger, despair and desolation burned a hole through his heart. For the next five months, every mission he was on, he'd pushed to the very limits of sanity, taking point, rushing headfirst into dangerous situations, taking out every enemy combatant he'd encountered, with no remorse. He hadn't eaten right, and sleep had been hard to come by unless he ran himself into the ground and passed out. He couldn't go fast enough, or far enough, to get away from the memory of Sandy dying in his arms.

By the time he and his team had redeployed back to the States, he'd lost twenty pounds and was having recurring nightmares, destroying what little sleep he managed to get. His team worried so much they reported him to his commanding officer.

When the CO called him into his office, he'd ordered him to see a shrink.

What good was a shrink? He couldn't bring Sandy back, nor could he bring back even one of the twenty-seven people who'd died in that marketplace.

Chance's reenlistment had come up, and he'd chosen to leave the Army and the unit that had been his family for so long. Haunted by memories he couldn't erase, he'd come back to Hellfire, hoping to find solace at home.

A soft whinny sounded from the other side of the stall door, jerking Chance back to the present. He glanced into the stall, looking for the occupant and didn't see one.

Another whinny made Chance frown.

"Look closer. He's really small," his sister said from behind him. "It's a miniature horse."

Chance opened the stall door and stared down at a horse the size of a large dog. Still deep in his memories, he struggled to form words. "When?" was all he could choke out.

"I brought Dexter home today. The poor little guy was being sold at auction. One of the glue factory guys was bidding on him. I couldn't let him go to him." Lily knelt beside the little horse and wrapped her arms around his neck. "He deserves to live a long life, not to end up as dog food or glue." She scratched behind the little horse's ears. "Isn't that right, Dexter?"

The horse tossed his head as though he understood and agreed with her.

Lily snapped a lead on his miniature halter and straightened. "I'm going to let him out in the pasture. He could use some exercise. Want to come with me?"

"No," Chance said. He wasn't good company at that moment.

Lily touched his arm. "You know we all love you, don't you?"

Chance's throat tightened, and his eyes burned. He nodded.

"Whatever happened on your last assignment…" Lily looked up into her brother's eyes. "Whatever it was…we're always here for you."

He pulled her into a quick hug. "Thanks."

She gave him a tight smile and led Dexter out to the paddock closest to the barn, opened the gate and unclipped the lead from his halter.

The little horse nuzzled her hand for a moment then kicked up his heels and raced across the grass.

If only it was that easy to let go of the bad things that had happened and embrace the new life he was living, far away from the dust of the desert.

Chance left the barn and walked to the fence to watch Dexter reveling in his newfound freedom. He had a lot he could learn from the antics of the miniature horse. If only he was open to the lesson.

CHAPTER 4

KATE AND BACCHUS stood on the porch as the family congratulated the couple upon the announcement of their engagement. For a moment, she considered slipping away, climbing into her truck and driving back to town.

As she turned to do just that, the woman who'd met her with Nash stepped up beside her. "I'm so happy for them. They went through a pretty rough time. They deserve all the happiness they can grab."

Curious, Kate asked, "Rough time?"

Phoebe nodded. "I wasn't here when it happened, but Kinsey's ex-boyfriend was abusive. She escaped him and came back home to get away. He followed her and tried to kill her. If he couldn't have her, he didn't want anyone else to have her." Phoebe's brow dipped. "That bastard. Who could hurt a sweetheart like Kinsey?"

Kate wouldn't know. She didn't know any of the people there. She didn't respond to the rhetorical question, standing in silence as the others continued their celebratory hugs and exclamations.

"Nash was happy to get another deputy in the department. They've been short-handed for a while now. Having you on the staff will take some of the pressure off the other deputies."

"I hope to come up to speed quickly," Kate said.

"I'm sure you will." She bent to Bacchus and paused before touching. "May I? He won't bite, will he?"

"Not unless I tell him to," Kate said.

Phoebe looked up, her eyes wide.

Kate smiled. "Don't worry. I won't tell him to."

"What's his name?" Phoebe asked as she ruffled the dog's neck.

"Bacchus."

"A handsome name for a handsome dog." She ran her hand along his back. "I understand he hired on with you." Phoebe straightened. "How's that going to work?"

"He was trained to sniff bombs. I'll be working to retrain him to sniff for drugs."

"Is it easy to retrain a dog?" Phoebe asked.

"He's smart. I think he'll catch on quickly." Kate hoped he would prove to be useful. Otherwise, the sheriff might decide to have her keep him at home instead of going along with her on her shift.

Now that she had Bacchus, she wanted him to be with her always. He was like her lifeline. As much as she thought she calmed him, he made her feel calm as well. And right at this moment in her life, he was her only friend.

"He's really smart," Kate repeated. "He'll learn."

"I'm sure he will." When Nash waved his hand toward her, Phoebe smiled. "Excuse me. I think I need to help Nash with the grill. Everyone seems to have forgotten the steaks."

Bacchus left her side and dropped down the steps to the ground.

"Where are you going, boy?" Kate asked, following the dog, figuring he was after the scent of the steaks on the grill. But when he passed the grill and continued toward the barn, Kate hurried after him, thinking she probably should have snapped his lead on before getting him out of the truck. She trusted that Bacchus would come to her command, but there were a lot of new and interesting things for him to sniff. He might get distracted.

He stopped in front of a gate and stuck his nose between the wooden slats.

Another nose met his.

Kate knelt beside Bacchus and peered through the gate at what appeared to be a horse. Only this horse was so tiny, it looked like a dog. She reached through the fence to pat its velvety nose. The little horse nibbled at her fingers. "Hi there." She wished she had a treat for the animal.

Bacchus sniffed at the little guy's face.

The horse tossed his head and touched his nose to Bacchus's.

Kate laughed. "You've made a friend." Which was more than she could say for herself. But it was a start.

"Are you a baby or some kind of dwarf?" Kate wondered aloud.

"He's a miniature horse, fully grown," a voice said behind her. "His name is Dexter."

Recognizing the voice, Kate jerked to her feet, spun and stumbled backward.

Chance grabbed her around the waist and steadied her. "Sorry. I didn't mean to frighten you."

She trembled, but not from fear of the man but of her body's reaction to his nearness. Her breath caught and held in her lungs as her chest pressed against his.

For a long moment, Chance held her, and time seemed to stand still. He was so close, she could feel the warmth of his minty breath against her cheeks.

Without realizing it, Kate swept her tongue across her lips.

Chance's gaze dropped from her eyes to her mouth. For a very brief moment, his blue eyes flared, and his head dipped lower.

Kate thought he was about to kiss her. Her pulse

quickened, and her heartbeat fluttered against her ribs.

The little horse reared and trotted away, the sound of its tiny hooves breaking through the trance.

"I wasn't so much frightened as s-startled," she said, appalled at how wispy her voice sounded to her own ears.

Chance straightened and dropped his arms.

Without his support, Kate's knees nearly buckled. She quickly locked them and stepped away, out of reach of his strong arms and the subtle scent of his cologne.

Dragging her gaze away from his, she shifted focus to the miniature horse trotting back up to the gate.

Once again, Bacchus touched noses with the animal.

"I didn't know horses came in compact sizes," Kate said, glad for the distraction. She willed her pulse to return to normal as she stood beside the tall firefighter.

"Have you been around ranch animals much?"

She gave a strained laugh. "I grew up in Texas, but this is my first time on a real, honest-to-goodness working ranch." Kate glanced toward him. "I'm from San Antonio. I guess you could say I'm a city girl, but I like to go on hikes, and I'm not afraid of physical work."

Chance nodded. "Especially if you made it

through boot camp and trained dogs while on active duty."

She nodded. "Exactly. I'm not completely inept in the outdoors. I fired expert on the M4A1 rifle, the .38, M9 and .45."

"I'm impressed," he said. His voice lowered, "Have you ever had to shoot someone with any one of those?"

A chill rippled across her skin. "No. But if I had to, I would. Why do you ask?"

Bacchus walked over to Chance, sat at his feet and looked up at him as if wondering the same.

Kate wanted to pat him on the back, but the dog was just out of her reach. Instead, she lifted her chin and waited for Chance's response.

"Hellfire might be a sleepy little town, but we've had our share of crime. If someone needed your help, and the situation required you to shoot a bad guy to save an innocent's life…"

"I'd shoot his ass," Kate stated firmly.

Chance chuckled. "Hopefully, shooting a man in the ass would slow him down enough."

Her eyebrows pulled downward. "You know what I mean."

He nodded, and then changed the subject. "Have you ever ridden a horse?"

Kate shook her head. "Never."

"Would you like to?"

She shrugged. "I suppose." Her gaze went to the

miniature horse, her eyes rounding. "You aren't suggesting we ride Dexter, are you?"

He laughed out loud. "No. Of course not." He tipped his head toward the barn. "We have larger horses for riding."

"In that case, I'd love to learn." She glanced toward Bacchus.

"He can come, too. The horses are used to having dogs around. We just lost our old hound dog last year."

"Just so you know, I heard what your family was saying as I walked out onto the deck a little while ago," Kate said.

Chance stiffened. "They mean well. I'm just not a good candidate for their matchmaking."

"And I wanted you to know, neither am I. I'd like to learn how to ride a horse from you…as a friend. Not a date."

"Good. Because I didn't mean it to sound like a date."

"Good." Now that she was clear, Kate couldn't think of anything else that needed to be said, other than, "When?"

"I'm on a twenty-four-hour shift tomorrow. It will have to be Tuesday or Wednesday."

"I'll have to work around my assigned work schedule at the sheriff's department."

"Then I'll wait to hear what you can do before we

make a date." He held up his hands. "Not a date. A plan." He held out his hand. "As friends."

She hesitated a moment before placing her hand in his. "Friends," she said with a little more force than necessary. Was she emphasizing the word for his benefit or for hers?

A LOUD CLANGING signaled dinner was ready. The sound brought back memories for Chance. He and his brothers had stayed outside all summer and after school until dark, unless their mother rang the bell for meals. Then they'd come running from all around to eat the wonderful, hearty meals she or his father had prepared. The two had loved cooking together when time permitted. Good memories.

Chance turned to Kate with a wry grin. "I bet you've never heard a dinner bell like that ring."

She laughed. "No. I can't say I have."

Chance stared up at the ranch house, dreading the not-so-subtle ribbing he expected from his siblings and the constant reminder that he needed to find someone to love from his parents. "Are you ready to face the family and their good intentions again?"

Kate drew in a deep breath and let it out. "For one of those steaks, I'd face a pack of bears." She rubbed her flat belly. "I'm hungry."

"Good, because between my mother and father,

they usually make enough food to feed a small army." He waved a hand toward the house. "Shall we?"

Kate fell in step with Chance. She glanced at the back porch where Mrs. Grayson stood near a cast iron bell. "We probably should have approached the house from different directions."

Chance frowned, his gaze on his family members. "Yeah. But it's too late now. They'll try to throw us together at every possible opening." He glanced down at her. "We could skip dinner and make a run for it."

She chuckled. "Don't tempt me. I would if I wasn't so hungry and the smell of charbroiled steak wasn't making my mouth water."

"Then steak and friendly harassment, it is." Chance marched her into the middle of his family. A long picnic table had been set out on the lawn and covered with a red, checkered tablecloth. The side dishes had been placed in the middle and covered with dish towels. Paper plates stood in a stack next to the forks, spoons, knives and condiments.

The men stood back, allowing the women to go first.

Chance's mother took the lead and filled her plate. She set it on the table, covered it with a napkin and ran back into the house for something she'd forgotten. Chance couldn't remember a time when Ann Grayson managed to get everything out on the table the first time. She always ran to the kitchen for some overlooked dish, steak sauce or pitcher of lemonade.

All of his brothers and their girls had taken their seats at the table by the time Chance got there, leaving only two spaces for him and Kate next to each other.

"See what I mean?" he whispered to Kate.

"A conspiracy, for sure," she whispered back. "Bacchus, *sitz*," she commanded.

Bacchus dropped his butt to the ground where he stood.

Lily glanced up from her seat at the table. "You have to teach me how to do that. When I move off the ranch, I want a dog to keep me company."

"When will that be, dear?" Chance's mother asked.

"What?" Lily raised her hands palms up. "You just got back to the ranch, and you're ready for me to leave?"

"The school year's almost over," his mother said. "I imagine you'll be off on some summer adventure as an au pair."

Lily nodded. "I've had a few inquiries."

"You work as an au pair?" Kate settled in the seat beside Lily and scooted over, making room for Chance.

"I work a regular school year at the elementary school, and then offer my services for the summer as an au pair." Lily reached for the bowl of potato salad and scooped a big dollop onto her paper plate.

"Preferably with a family that likes to travel to new and exotic places. That way, I get to see more of the world on someone else's dime, and I'm getting paid as well."

"Don't you get tired of babysitting other people's children?" Becket asked.

Lily shrugged. "Not really. So far, families allow me a budget to take the children sightseeing or to the beach. The children have, for the most part, been good and easy to work with. It's a perfect way to spend my summer." She passed the potato salad to Kate and grinned. "And I get one day off each week to do what I want. It works for me while I'm still single, footloose and fancy-free."

"What about you, Kate?" Chance's mother turned the attention to the woman beside him. "What brings you to such a small town?"

Kate scooped potato salad onto her plate and handed the bowl to Chance before answering, "The job."

"Nash said you're from San Antonio," Big John noted. "Couldn't you have gone to work for the SAPD?"

She shook her head. "One of my stipulations for taking this position was that Bacchus was part of the deal."

The dog's head lifted a little higher, and his ears perked as if he knew they were talking about him.

"You'd think the San Antonio Police Department

would want a dog like Bacchus in its canine division," Becket said.

Kate's lips pressed together. "Most people think MWDs are useless once retired. Bacchus's only quirk was he got skittish when confronted with loud noises. He was a bomb-sniffing dog. I think he can be trained to sniff for drugs."

"I know the department couldn't afford to send a dog to get that kind of training. Having a dog handler on staff will be an asset," Nash said. "I wouldn't mind learning some of your skills, as well."

"You're more than welcome to tag along when I'm training," Kate offered.

Chance had never wanted to be a deputy...up until that moment. He liked fighting fires and being an emergency medical technician, helping people when they needed him most. But he found himself wishing he had the option of working with Kate in her effort to retrain Bacchus to sniff for drugs.

He told himself it was because he liked dogs and was interested in how to train them, but he'd be lying. Kate interested him in a way no woman had captured his interest since Sandy's death.

"You going to hold the potato salad all day or let the rest of us have some?" his father asked.

Startled out of his musings, Chance dug the big spoon into the bowl, ladled out a heaping helping and passed the bowl across the table to his father. "Sorry."

"What's got you wool-gathering, son?" his father asked as he helped himself to the contents of the bowl.

"Nothing," he answered, perhaps a little too quickly.

"I think he's sitting next to what's on his mind," Lily said as she stabbed a fork into a juicy steak on the platter being passed around the table.

"Don't go there," Chance warned. "You heard me earlier. I don't need your help finding a woman to fill my life. My life if full enough as it is."

Kate smiled. "And though it's flattering that you might consider me a candidate for the position of Chance's woman, I just got out of a messy relationship. I've sworn off dating for a while."

"Then that makes you perfect for each other," Lily declared. "Isn't it always when you're not looking that you find that perfect someone?"

"Lily," Chance glared at his sister.

She pressed her lips together and pulled an imaginary zipper across them. "Not saying another word."

"Yeah," Rider snorted. "Like you can keep your mouth shut for an entire minute."

"Shut up, Rider. I can and will." Lily cut off a piece of her steak and shoved it into her mouth.

"Only because you're eating," Rider muttered and turned to Chance. "Keep feeding her, and you might get some peace to finish your meal."

Chance shook his head. "What would we do without family to embarrass us in front of guests?"

"Be a lot happier," Becket said between bites of his steak.

Kinsey elbowed him in the side. "You don't mean that. You are so lucky to have a family who loves you enough to care whether you're happy or not." She leaned toward Chance. "They only want you to be happy."

"My life is fine the way it is," Chance said. "Why screw it up by forcing me into a relationship?"

"Ha!" Lily pointed at him. "You didn't say you were happy. You said your life is fine."

"So?' Chance frowned.

"'Fine' is that word you use when things are anything but fine." Lily crossed her arms over her chest. "And you're too thick-headed to admit you aren't happy."

Chance opened his mouth to tell his little sister that he was happy, but the words wouldn't come. He wasn't happy and hadn't been since Sandy had died. He couldn't out-and-out lie about it. "Happiness is all relative. I don't like to get too excited, because every time I do, something awful happens, and I'm knocked back on my ass. If I don't let myself get too happy, I don't have as far to fall when I'm knocked down."

"But life is short," Chance's mother said, her forehead wrinkling. "You have to grab all the happiness and sunshine you can to help you weather the darker parts of your life on this earth." She reached out a hand to her husband. "Our life hasn't always been sunshine and roses."

"No, dear, it hasn't." Big John lifted his wife's hand and pressed a kiss to the back of her knuckles. "We had to work at it. But it was worth every bit of effort."

Chance's mother smiled. "Yes, it was." She returned her attention to her son. "I know how rewarding life with the one you love can be. You can't blame a mother for wanting the best for her sons and daughter."

"No, Mom, I can't. But give it time," Chance said with a soft smile. "If it's meant to happen, it will." He didn't mention that he'd lost his chance when Sandy died. If his mother needed to hold out hope that her children would all be married and raising their own children, then who was he to dash her hope? "You do have another child who remains unattached."

His mother's attention pivoted to Lily.

Lily held up her hands. "I'm too young to get married. I still have a whole world to see before I'm saddled with kids of my own."

"Lily, you're not too young," their mother said. "If you wait too long, you might miss your chance to have children."

"You were having children into your thirties," Lily pointed out.

"Yes, dear. I had you when I was thirty-two," she

said. "But not every woman is the same. Some have trouble getting pregnant in their thirties."

Lily frowned. "That argument isn't good enough for me to run out and find a baby daddy right this minute."

Her mother laughed. "Oh, sweetheart, I don't mean for you to run out and find anyone. I just want you to keep your options open. Just like I want Chance to do the same." She winked at Chance. "You won't know if the one you've been waiting for is right beside you, if you don't at least look around." She clapped her hands. "Enough of this talk. Who wants dessert?"

"Me," Rider said. "All this deep talk has given me a hell of a sweet tooth. And my sweetie isn't due back to Hellfire until the end of the spring semester." He stood and gathered the empty plates around him. "Did I see that you made pies?"

"I did," his mother replied with a grin. "Apple and pecan."

"I'm going for some of both," Rider announced. "Before the rest of you yahoos get it all."

Becket jumped up. "Last time you went first, there wasn't much left for the rest of us." He, too, gathered plates. "I'll bring the pies out here for Mom to cut."

"I'll help," Kinsey offered.

Soon, everyone was up and moving toward the kitchen.

Chance stood but didn't follow the others.

"Aren't you afraid you'll miss out on the pie?" Kate rose to stand beside him.

He shrugged. "Not really." Patting his belly, he drew in a deep breath. "I could stand to lose a few pounds."

Kate snorted. "Like you have a spare ounce of flesh on you." She frowned. "When did you get off active duty?"

"Two years ago."

Her eyebrows rose. "And you didn't immediately gain twenty pounds?" She shook her head. "I aspire to your dedication to fitness."

"Not dedication. Sometimes, I forget to eat."

Kate's lips twisted. "I've forgotten my wallet, left my keys in my car and forgotten to take out the trash, but I've never forgotten to eat."

Chance glanced across the pasture toward the last flare of the setting sun. "I keep busy."

"Too busy to fuel your body?"

"Sometimes," he said.

"Chance," Rider leaned out the back door. "You want a beer?"

Chance shook his head. "On duty tomorrow. I'll pass."

"What about you, Kate?" Rider asked.

She shook her head. "Sounds good, but I start my new job tomorrow. I'd rather do that without the hangover."

"Good. That leaves more for me." He winked and disappeared back inside.

Kate glanced at her watch. "I guess I'd better head back to my apartment. I still have to unpack and get organized."

"I need to get away from here for a little while. I can lead or follow to make sure you get there, if you like."

"You don't have to. I'm sure my GPS will get me back the same way I came."

"Trust me, I need to escape. I live here when I'm not at the station. Sometimes, you can get a little too much family for comfort. I really need to remedy that situation, soon, with a place of my own." His lips twisted into a wry grin. "I love my family and they love me, but right now, I need my space."

Kate nodded. "You're lucky you have a family as close-knit as yours." She glanced across the pasture. "Not everyone has that luxury."

"I know. However, sometimes, they…smother me." He ran a hand through his hair. "I just need to feel the wind in my face."

"If you're ready, so am I." Kate looked around at the table. "I need to thank your family for letting me crash the party."

"You didn't crash the party. You gave my parents and siblings a chance to give me hell. They appreciate any opportunity they can get." He chuckled. "Sorry they dragged you into their efforts at matchmaking."

"I'm flattered. It would be an honor to be a part of your family." She pushed a stray strand of hair back behind her ear. "I'm just not a good candidate at this time. I have trust issues after my recent break up."

"Sounds like your ex was a jerk."

"He was a piece of work. I won't go into the sordid details. Suffice it to say, he used me and kept a girlfriend on the side while I was deployed."

"Bastard."

"Yeah, but he's out of my life now. I'm much better off without him."

"True. If he couldn't remain faithful to you while you were deployed, he didn't deserve you."

"I agree." She drew in a deep breath and let it out. "Hellfire and my job with the sheriff's department are all part of the new me. I just hope the transition from military to civilian life is smooth. How was it for you?"

"I'm not your poster child for a smooth transition. It's been two years since I got out, but it doesn't feel like it's been that long."

"PTSD?"

He shrugged. "If PTSD is nightmares, yes."

"I'm sorry." Kate touched his arm.

A shock of awareness ripped through his arm and into his chest. "Don't be. It's my problem. I'll get over it."

"A lot of soldiers try to muscle their way through the transition and fail," Kate pointed out.

Chance stiffened. "I'm fine."

"That's what they all say until they can't handle it anymore and commit suicide." She shook her head. "Have you seen a therapist?"

"No," Chance said, hoping she would drop the subject.

"Well, if you need anyone to talk to who understands the stress of deployment, I'm a good listener."

"Thanks. I don't need a shrink, and I don't need someone to listen to all of my problems. I'm fine without all that stuff. All I need is the wind in my face and a lot of road to travel."

Kate chuckled. "Sounds like a country-western song." She snapped her fingers. "*Fuss*, Bacchus," she said, giving the dog the command to heel.

The dog leaped up from where he'd been lying in the cool dirt of the flower bed. He came to stand beside Kate.

"Ready to go to our new home?" she asked.

Bacchus woofed.

The gentle smile on Kate's face melted through the hardness in Chance's heart. "You should smile more often," he said softly.

Kate looked up into his eyes. "I plan on it."

Chance hoped she followed through with her plan. Just because he didn't find much to smile about, didn't mean Kate couldn't have a full and happy life in Hellfire.

As he followed her through the house to give her

thanks for the meal and company, he couldn't help thinking this woman had her life in order. He found himself wanting to be in that very same place in his own life.

Perhaps, it was time to let go of the survivor's guilt. Sandy wouldn't have wanted him to go through the rest of his life mourning her death or wishing it had been him instead.

If she could visit him from the other side of eternity, she'd tell him to live life to the fullest. Fall in love. Have a family. Grow roots.

He followed Kate all the way into town, remembering how the new deputy had felt in his arms. Warm, soft in all the right places and smelling of spring flowers and sunshine. Being near her made him forget Sandy and what they'd had. If only for a moment.

His mother would call that progress, and she'd likely try set him up with the pretty new deputy. He agreed he needed to get on with his life. But Kate wasn't interested, and Chance wasn't that ready to choose another woman. He could use a friend, though.

Kate was interesting, loved dogs and wanted to make Hellfire her home.

As a firefighter working long shifts, he had a lot of time off between them. Perhaps instead of riding his dirt bike on dangerous trails, he might learn more about training dogs.

CHAPTER 5

KATE PULLED into the driveway of the garage apartment and shifted into park. Part of her wanted Chance to stop and get off his motorcycle. The smart woman, who'd just gotten out of a toxic relationship, wanted him to drive by with a wave and leave her alone.

Chance pulled up behind her, swung his leg over the seat and levered the kickstand into place. He nodded his helmet-clad head toward the charred remains of Lola's house. "They should start cleaning up the debris soon. Lola had to wait for the insurance adjuster to work his magic, and then the contractor to give her a quote."

"Will she rebuild?"

Chance nodded. "I hear she will." He grinned. "She and one of my firefighter buddies are going to design and build the house of their dreams."

Kate stared at the blackened nubs that had once been the foundation of a home. "Kind of like a phoenix rising from the ashes."

Chance nodded, a smile pulling at the corners of his lips. "Never thought Daniel would find the love of his life in Lola Engel. But now that they're together, it makes sense."

"How so?"

He shrugged. "I don't know. They just fit." He started toward the stairs leading up to the apartment.

"I can take it from here," she called after him.

"Call me old-fashioned, but I'd feel better if I made sure your apartment is safe."

"Why wouldn't it be?" She glanced around at the quiet Main Street. "I thought small town living was all about leaving doors unlocked and trusting everyone."

Chance tipped his head toward the burned-out hull of a house. "Even small towns have crime. Lola almost died in that house."

Kate pushed aside the ripple of unease snaking across her skin. "I hired on as a deputy. I have to be able to handle any situation."

She could see Chance's jaw tighten in the dim glow of the street light. "I'm here. You might as well let me check it out. I promise, I won't stay. Call it part of my PTSD I'm working through. I need to know you're safe."

Kate stared at him hard, trying to read into his

words to understand his need to see her safely inside her apartment. What had happened during his deployment that had made him so adamant about seeing to her wellbeing? Finally, she waved her hand toward the apartment stairs. "Knock yourself out."

Chance took the steps two at a time without breathing hard by the time he reached the top.

Kate followed at a slightly slower pace with Bacchus behind her. When she reached the top landing, Chance held out his hand for her key. Once he had it in his hand, he opened the door, pushed it inward and flipped on the light switch.

The apartment wasn't much more than a single room with a kitchenette in one corner, a bed in another corner, a couch and coffee table and a wardrobe to hang her clothes in. A small room at the back was the tiny bathroom with a narrow shower, just big enough for one person.

Chance walked to that closed door, poked his head inside for a second and closed it again.

"Not many places for a bogeyman to hide, are there?" Kate noted, from where she stood in the doorway.

"No." He wrinkled his nose. "I can still smell the smoke from the fire."

Kate nodded. "I was forewarned. But I'll air it out over the next few days. It will be fine." Better than the apartment she'd left behind in San Antonio that smelled of old pizza, dirty clothes and the muskiness of a mildewed bathroom.

Bacchus entered the apartment and sniffed at all the furnishings and in all the corners.

Chance crossed the room in three short steps and held out her keys.

Kate lifted her hand, palm up.

When he placed the keys in her open hand, his knuckles brushed against her skin, sending a shower of sparks through her nervous system.

Instead of jerking back her hand, she looked up into Chance's blue, smoldering gaze.

For a moment, he stared back into her eyes, his irises flaring. Then his brows descended. He gripped her arms and pulled her up against him. "Why?" he said, his voice ragged, as if drawn from someplace deep inside him. Someplace dark and tortured.

"Why what?" she asked, her words coming out in a breathy whisper. His hands on her arms were strong, forceful and commanding. With her breasts pressed against his hard chest, she couldn't help but feel the strength in the hardness of his muscles, and the tension radiating from his body into hers.

His head lowered toward her until his lips hovered an inch from hers. "Why am I feeling this?"

"Feeling what?" She knew damned well what he was feeling, because she was feeling it herself. But she wanted him to explain something she wasn't sure she could describe herself.

"I'm not available." He shook her gently. "Don't you see? I'm no good for anyone."

Kate frowned. "I don't expect you to be available." She raised her hands to balance on his waist as if to hold herself up should he release the hold he had on her arms.

"I can't do this," he muttered. Then he lowered his head and brushed his lips against hers.

What started as a light touch grew harder, until he ground his mouth against hers in a kiss so desperate, she could feel the internal pain driving it.

Her fingers curled into the fabric of his shirt. She had the thought of pushing him away, but her hands weren't cooperating. Instead, they were drawing him closer. She lifted up on her toes, deepening the kiss as if she didn't have any other option.

When he finally jerked his head up and dropped his hands to his sides, Chance stepped back and scrubbed a hand over his face. "I'm sorry. That shouldn't have happened."

Kate touched her fingers to her swollen lips, dazed, confused and on fire to her very core. "What just happened?"

He shook his head. "Nothing. Forget about it. It won't happen again." Chance pushed past her and out of the apartment, slamming the door behind him.

Kate stood in the exact spot where he'd kissed her, head spinning, the blood in her veins pulsing hard with the rapid beat of her heart.

Bacchus sat at her feet, looking up at her, his head tilted.

The sound of a motorcycle revving, drew Kate out of her stunned stupor and to the window overlooking the driveway.

Chance had pulled on his helmet and turned the bike around. The last thing Kate saw was the blur of his taillight as he tore out onto Main Street, headed the opposite direction from the ranch.

For a long time, she stared out the window at the dark, empty street, willing her pulse to slow to a normal rate. All the while, she asked herself, *What the hell just happened?*

CHANCE RACED OUT OF HELLFIRE, increasing his speed after he reached the edge of town until he was traveling well over ninety miles per hour. The road was straight for a long way, and he let the speed, the wind and the stars guide him.

What the hell had just happened?

He'd kissed a stranger he'd met only that day.

A dull, burning feeling hit him in the pit of his gut. Images of Sandy dying in his arms rolled through his memory like a video repeating over and over. He'd kissed a woman who wasn't Sandy.

And he'd liked it.

When he reached the road leading out to a small canyon, he slowed and turned onto the gravel. Then he sped up, not as fast as he'd been driving on the pavement, but fast enough he had to focus to keep from losing control. Even then, his mind was torn between dodging ruts, Sandy's dying breath and the warmth of Kate in his arms.

He weaved his way between trees and emerged into an open area, hitting the brakes in time to come to a skidding stop at the edge of the small canyon.

Stars shone down on a moonless night, providing enough light to bathe the rocky crevasse in a blue, shimmering light.

No matter what happened to those you loved, the stars managed to come out and keep shining. Nature had a way of continuing on, unremorseful or unaware of the lives lost.

Chance killed the engine, removed his helmet and breathed deeply, trying to calm his ravaged soul. Unlike the stars that managed to keep on shining, he couldn't move past the guilt, the regret and second-guessing that had accompanied him from the moment of Sandy's death until two years later, where he stood at the edge of a cliff, wondering what had just happened.

Was kissing Kate the first step in forgetting Sandy?

His gut knotted.

He couldn't forget Sandy. She would always be a part of who he was. But there was so much more. He couldn't stagnate in the past. Was that what he'd done by coming home? Was he trying to recapture the innocence and painlessness of his childhood? Should he have moved somewhere else to force himself to start over?

"What's the answer?" he called out.

His voice echoed off the walls of the canyon, coming back to him with the same question and no answer.

He swung his leg over the seat and walked to the edge. Some soldiers came back home, hoping to pick up their lives where they'd left off when they'd joined the military. But deployment and being a part of a war machine had changed who they were.

Chance wasn't the same person he'd been when he'd left Hellfire to join the Army. Coming back had proven that to him. He could have gone to work on the ranch but had signed on to become a firefighter instead, hoping the action and rescue calls would help take his mind off what he'd lost in that split-second of gunfire.

Though he loved being a firefighter and helping people in their time of need, he had too much time on his hands between calls. He'd found solace in working out, running on the treadmill, lifting weights, all the while listening to loud music on his headset. Anything to get his mind out of Afghanistan.

No matter how hard he pushed himself physically, he couldn't erase the sad memories of Sandy.

Maybe he was going about it all wrong. Instead of trying to erase those memories, he should have embraced the good ones and lived on for her. She'd always been so full of life and laughter. By wallowing in his grief, was he doing her memory a disservice? She would have been the first to tell him to get on with his life. She'd have told him that life was too short to be sad all the time. *Live it!* she would have said.

And he hadn't been living. Not really.

So what had the kiss been all about?

Sandy's image faded to the back of his mind as he pictured Kate standing there after he'd kissed her. She was nothing like Sandy. Kate was all dark where Sandy had been light. Where Sandy had been blond with blue eyes and pale skin, Kate had dark hair, green eyes and tanned skin. She was tall and athletic, compared to Sandy's slight figure and short stature. He was sure Kate could have knocked him on his ass if she'd felt insulted by the way he'd kissed her. But, hell, she'd kissed him back.

He touched a hand to his lips. Hell, he'd liked it far too much and would have gone on longer, if not for the guilt twisting a hole in his chest.

Kate was not Sandy.

She never would be.

Sandy had been small and feisty. But he'd felt the need to protect her, even though she'd gone through the same combat training he had. She would have been mad at him for it, but she would have loved him for caring.

Kate was... Well...hell...he didn't really know much about the woman, other than she liked dogs and was kind to animals, like the miniature horse out at the ranch.

And her kiss.

Chance blew out a heavy sigh, his heart conflicted, his head spinning with what had happened. What he'd *let* happen.

He could ignore it and the way his body had felt pressed against hers. His snort made a tiny echo against the canyon walls, mocking him.

His best bet was to avoid Kate Bradley and go back to living his life the way he'd lived it over the past two years.

Alone.

With his new resolve firmly in mind, he pushed the helmet back on, mounted his bike and drove back to the ranch. Tomorrow would be there all too soon, and he had a twenty-four-hour shift to work at the fire station. Thinking ahead, he planned out his day, free of any thoughts of Kate. He'd keep busy. Very busy, in order to forget the way her lips felt beneath his and the way her soft, warm breasts pressed against his hard chest.

Yeah, he'd have to lift a lot of weights and wash all the trucks in the bay to keep those thoughts from slipping into his mind.

. . .

KATE SPENT the next hour unpacking her few belongings and placing them in the drawers and wardrobe. She'd opened all of the windows, searching for a cool night breeze to help lessen the smell of old smoke inside the small space. After a while, she couldn't really smell the charred scent. Either she was getting used to it, or the breeze was doing its job.

When she'd done all she could do to prepare herself for the next day and the start of her new job, she lay on the clean sheets of the full-sized bed and closed her eyes.

Bacchus lay on his pallet on the floor beside her, instantly asleep.

Kate envied the dog's ability to pass out so quickly.

Sounds drifted through the open window. A vehicle passed slowly on the street below, a dog barked in the distance and a couple of cats got into a fight nearby. An hour later, the rumble of a motorcycle engine passed on the street. Kate's eyes opened as she wondered if it was Chance on his way back through town.

She gave up trying to sleep and sat up. Perhaps if she counted all of her blessings, she'd have enough to get her to sleep. She'd learned to count her blessings instead of sheep from her mother, who'd been a big fan of old musical movies. She'd sing her the song

Count Your Blessings that Bing Crosby had sung to Rosemary Clooney in *White Christmas*.

Thoughts of her mother always made Kate smile. Though she'd died younger than she should have of breast cancer, she'd made Kate promise to remember the good times, not the sadness of her passing. Settling back against the pillow, she closed her eyes again.

Now, as she lay in a new town full of strangers, she tried to think through all the good things in her life, pushing the bad shit to the background.

She had Bacchus. The dog had been her lifeline during their training and deployments. He wasn't just a government issue, Military War Dog. He was her friend and part of her family of two. Kate and Bacchus.

She could be sad about having only one other being in her life, but she focused on the good. She had Bacchus when it could have been a difficult transition from retiring the dog to securing permission to take him with her upon leaving the military. Her letter to her congressman had helped in her appeal to adopt Bacchus. She was truly blessed to have her friend in her life.

She had a job. Transitioning from military to civilian life could have been so much more difficult. Fate had made her look online at the exact right time to find the advertisement for the sheriff's deputy position in Hellfire, Texas. She'd applied at once and received an answer within days. She hadn't been able to interview in person but had managed to find a way to perform the interview using her internet tablet and an application that allowed her to see her new boss and for him to see her. Technology had worked wonders for her in this instance. Sheriff Olson had been impressed with her drive and determination, so much so, he'd offered her the job and ultimately granted her special condition upon employment. Bacchus would be her sidekick to be retrained to handle some police work.

She'd met some wonderful people upon arriving in Hellfire and had a great meal with a nice family. Kate smiled at this blessing. She couldn't have asked for a better introduction to some of the residents of the county.

Those three blessings alone were pretty great.

What about the last one? A little voice in her head poked at her musings.

Kate closed her eyes again and willed the memory away. But it wasn't going anywhere. Not when her lips still throbbed and her core heated every time she thought about it.

That kiss.

She'd vowed to keep men at a distance for a long time. After the hassle of booting Randy out of her apartment, she didn't want to go through that kind of drama all over again.

She'd gone months without someone to hold her

and kiss her. During deployment, fraternizing with another soldier had been strictly forbidden. Not that she'd been tempted. She wouldn't break the rules, nor would she cheat on Randy when she hadn't broken off their relationship. Even had she known he was cheating on her, she hadn't met anyone who came close to tempting her.

How long could she go without someone to hold her, kiss her and make love to her?

She clenched her fists. She hadn't even thought she needed to be held until Chance had pulled her into his arms, and then surprised her with a kiss.

Damn him to hell.

He'd awakened in her a need she hadn't known she had. Why couldn't he have just left her at the curb and driven away? He'd only managed to complicate her life. Hellfire was supposed to be a fresh start, a chance to cleanse her spirit of bad memories and failed relationships.

Chance Grayson had potential-failed-relationship written all over him.

CHAPTER 6

CHANCE TOSSED and turned until the wee hours of the morning when he finally fell asleep and dreamed. In his dreams, he knelt beside a woman who lay crumpled on the hard desert ground. When he turned her over, it wasn't Sandy but a dark-haired, green-eyed beauty who stared back at him.

Shocked by the image, he muttered, "You?"

"Yes, me," she said.

"Why?"

"Because I'm still here. She's not."

"But you're not her," he said.

"No. I'm not. And I never will be. But I'm me. And I'm here." The sand beneath her turned to flowing white sheets. They were in a bed, naked and alone.

She reached up, wound her arms around his neck and pulled him down to kiss her.

He couldn't fight the desire and didn't want to.

This was what he wanted. She was alive, warm and real in his arms.

The shrill ringing of his alarm jerked him out of the dream. Chance sat up and looked around, expecting to see Kate lying in the bed beside him.

It took him a full minute to realize he was by himself. The pillow on the other side of the bed had no indentation. It had never been slept on. The heat radiating through his body cooled to normal in the air-conditioned room.

He scrubbed a hand over his face, threw aside the comforter and swung his legs out of bed. With only thirty minutes to get fed, dressed and to work, he had to get moving.

A cool shower further helped to chill the desire he'd manifested in his dream. When he emerged, he felt closer to his normal self. He wondered what a therapist would say about his dream. Had his guilt over kissing another woman brought that woman into his dreams to mock him? Or had his memories of Sandy begun to fade and meeting Kate only helped him let go a little faster?

He didn't want to forget Sandy. She should have been with him coming back from deployment. They should have been married by now and maybe have a kid on the way.

But she wasn't, and no amount of second-guessing what he should have done that day would bring her back. He had to get on with his life. Without Sandy.

Skipping breakfast, he dressed in his uniform and boots and hurried through the ranch house to the door.

"Hey, where's my hug and a kiss?" his mother asked from the kitchen.

"Gonna be late for work," he said, but swerved toward the kitchen to hug and kiss his mother. "Love you, Mom. Hope you and Dad will be home for a while."

"Oh, we aren't going anywhere. At least for another month or so." She smiled at him. "Here's to hoping for a boring shift."

Chance's mouth twisted. "Thanks, Mom."

"You know what I mean. If there aren't any fires, no one is getting hurt or losing everything they own."

"I know, Mom. I wish for the same. But sometimes, it's nice to be able to save someone in need."

"You adrenaline junkies. You'd probably be better off working for the fire department in a bigger city like Dallas or Austin." She sighed. "But I'm glad you came home to Hellfire."

"Me, too." He hugged her again. "Gotta go." Then he ran out the door, jumped on his bike and headed into Hellfire, not slowing until he reached the edge of town.

As he cruised down Main Street, he shifted into a lower gear, passing by Lola's garage apartment. If he crept past even slower at that point, he could say he'd seen a cat and didn't want to hit it. He didn't see any sign of the new deputy. It was well before the time she was due to start her shift at the sheriff's department. She probably wasn't even awake yet.

He wondered if she'd slept better than he had. Had she lain in bed until the early hours of the morning thinking about the kiss? Or had she been angry with him for stepping over the line she'd drawn in the sand when she'd said she wasn't interested in a relationship?

Chance pulled into the station, parked his motorcycle and entered through the open bay where the two guys on the previous shift, Big Mike Sandoval and Jace Kelly, were cleaning a stretcher and restocking the medical bag.

"Figures you'd get here about now," Mike said as he tucked the hose in position and locked it down. "Bones just said breakfast would be ready in five minutes."

"Perfect timing, if you ask me," Chance said and shoved his helmet into the cubby next to the door leading into the station. "Need a hand?"

"Nah," Jace said. "We just got back from a lift assist."

"Any action last night?"

"Just the lift assist and a kitchen grease fire," Big Mike said.

Chance chuckled. "Sounds like you caught up on

your sleep."

"Which is more than we can say for you, based on the dark circles beneath your eyes." Big Mike joined him at the door and clapped a meaty hand on his shoulder. "Pull an all-nighter at the Ugly Stick Saloon?"

Chance snorted. "I wish. No. Just couldn't get to sleep." He pushed through the door and entered the fire station.

"Thinking about the new chick in town?" Jace asked, bringing up the rear. "I hear you met the sheriff's new hire."

"She's not a chick," Chance muttered.

"No? I thought I heard the sheriff hired the county's first female deputy."

"She's female, all right. But have a little respect."

"Yeah, Kelly." Big Mike backhanded Jace in the belly. "I hear she's tough. Prior service, Army. I imagine she could kick your ass all over town."

Jace frowned. "Doubt it."

Big Mike laughed. "If not her, her dog could take you down."

Chance ignored their banter, not wanting to talk about the latest female addition to Hellfire's population. He'd thought about her far too much through the night. As he passed by a window looking out over Main Street, a streak of feminine curves passed, accompanied by a dog.

His paused, his pulse quickening.

"Speak of the devil, and she appears, as if by magic," said Big Mike.

Jace whistled. "That's her? I'm feeling like I need to break at least a half-dozen laws if she's on duty today."

Chance glared at the younger firefighter. "Back off, Kelly. She just got out of a bad relationship. She's not interested in starting a new one."

Big Mike's eyebrows rose. "You seem to know a lot about her already. Sounds like you made a pass at her and got shot down."

Heat burned a path up into Chance's cheeks. He couldn't deny the statement. He hadn't asked her if he could kiss her. But then, she hadn't struggled to get away. In fact, she'd leaned in to deepen the pressure. Heat spread lower into his groin. "None of your business."

Mike and Jace were laughing as they entered the station's kitchen.

"What's the joke?" Braden 'Bones' McCrae stood at the gas stove, stirring fluffy yellow eggs in a skillet.

"Our man Grayson's staked his claim on the new deputy in town."

"No, I haven't," Chance corrected. "I only said she's not interested in dating right now."

"But you want to be the first in line when she's ready, right?" Big Mike laughed. "Glad to see you rejoining the human race, Grayson."

"Me, too." Bones turned to scoop scrambled eggs into a large bowl.

"What do you mean, rejoin the human race? I've been here all along." Chance grabbed plates from the cabinet and set them out on the table.

Daniel Flannigan entered the kitchen. "Who's been here all along?"

"I have." Chance jerked his head toward the others in the room. "These guys don't know what they're talking about."

"Flannigan will agree with us." Jace crossed his arms over his chest. "Ain't that right?"

Daniel grabbed a mug and poured it full of steaming coffee. "What am I agreeing to?"

"That Chance has been checked out of the human race." Big Mike tossed several forks on the table and pulled up a chair. "Up until today."

Chance cringed.

Daniel's eyebrows rose up his forehead. "I'm off a couple days, and my buddy rejoined the human race? Do tell. What's happening? Is this about the new deputy in town?"

Chance sank into a chair and braced himself for the good-natured ribbing he had to endure until the previous shift left. "It must have been a boring night, if all you have to entertain yourselves is harassing me."

"We aren't harassing," Jace said. "We were discussing your love life."

"Damn, Grayson, when did you get a love life? And you didn't tell me about it?" Daniel shook his head and reached for the bowl of scrambled eggs Bones was setting in the middle of the table.

"There's nothing to tell," Chance insisted. "I don't have a love life. I'm not interested in the new deputy and these guys must have been smoking dope on shift. Isn't it about time to do a drug test?" Daniel passed him the bowl of scrambled eggs.

"You get the feeling he's protesting too much?" Big Mike slipped several slices of bacon onto his plate.

Chance helped himself to the eggs and then the bacon and poured juice into his glass. "Don't you have something more interesting to talk about than me? Flannigan how's Lola?"

"She's due back from Dallas tomorrow."

"What's she doing there?" Chance asked, trying his best to keep the conversation steered away from him and Kate.

"Some shoe convention," Daniel said between bites of his food. "Has to do with stocking her shoe store for the next season's sales."

"Have you two decided on a plan for the house you're going to build?" Chance asked.

"We're getting close. I told her I'm not moving in until we put a ring on it."

"On the house?" Chance asked, acting dumb, knowing exactly what his friend was talking about.

"On her finger, dumbass." Daniel frowned at him.

Jace's eyebrows lifted. "Is that how you asked her to marry you?" He lowered his voice to what Daniel's sounded like. "Hey, babe, I'm not moving in until I put a ring on it." Jace laughed. "I'm sure she said yes with a proposal like that."

"No, I did it right."

Big Mike pinned him with a glance. "On one knee?"

Daniel nodded.

"With a big fat diamond?" Kelly asked.

Daniel's face suffused a ruddy red. "As big as I could afford."

Big Mike frowned. "So, it was small."

"No, but it wasn't a huge rock."

Chance stopped eating long enough to study his friend. "And she said no?"

"She said yes, but…"

"But?" Big Mike shook his head. "That doesn't bode well."

"But she wants to wait to get married until the house is done."

"Why?"

"She wants to start our life together in the new house, not living in my dumpy trailer or the back of her shoe shop like she is now."

"Damn, who would have thought Lola Engel would turn out to be a woman who made sense?" Jace grinned.

Daniel glared at the younger man. "Watch it, Kelly."

"After all the times she cried wolf to get Chance out to rescue her, you'd think she was an airhead."

"Kelly…" Daniel growled low in his throat.

Jace shrugged. "Well, she did. She was after Chance."

Chance grinned. "But she fell for Flannigan instead."

"It's a great story, if you ask me." Big Mike smiled.

"Anyway, this conversation didn't start around me and Lola." Daniel turned to Chance. "We were discussing the new deputy. What's this about you having a thing for Kate Bradley?"

Chance groaned, stuffed the rest of his food into his mouth and leaped to his feet. "Breakfast's over. I'll do the dishes."

"You can run, but you can't hide. If there's anything going on between you and the deputy, it'll be all over town by lunch."

"There isn't," Chance said. "Drop it."

Daniel nodded, his calculating gaze on his Chance. "Uh huh. Yeah. We'll see."

Great. By noon, the whole town would think he and Kate were having a torrid love affair. God, he hoped she didn't slug him the next time they met. He finished the dishes and hurried out to the bay where they kept the weight equipment. Pumping iron burned off energy, and suddenly he had more energy than he could deal with. Thoughts of Kate and her soft lips beneath his kept flashing through his mind. He had to do something to get a grip on reality.

She wasn't interested, and he wasn't going to pursue her.

KATE HADN'T SLEPT WELL. By five o'clock in the morning, she'd given up on sleep and had risen to perform her morning yoga, sit-ups and pushups. Then she had breakfast, watched the news and still had energy to burn.

Bacchus had been a good sport about living in the confines of the tiny apartment, but he needed exercise, too.

Kate had pulled on her gym shorts and a tank top, tied on her running shoes and snapped the lead on Bacchus's collar. The best way to get to know a town was to get out and walk or jog the streets. A few minutes later, she'd been out the door and jogging down Main Street, passing in front of the fire station. The bay door had been open and she'd seen the trucks lined up inside, but no one standing around.

For a moment, she'd felt something akin to disappointment. So, Chance hadn't been hanging around where she could catch a glimpse of him. She attributed her disappointment to the fact he was one of only a few familiar faces she knew in town. Wanting to see a familiar face was her reason for hoping to see his. Not the fact that he'd kissed her the night before.

No. She wasn't interested in seeing where another kiss might lead. She'd sworn off men for the next few months. After being cooped up for most of the previous day's move, Bacchus seemed to enjoy getting out and running alongside Kate.

They made their way past the northern edge of town and out into the countryside for a couple miles before Kate turned around. On the way back through Hellfire, Kate swung into side streets, weaving her way into little neighborhoods of quaint houses and back out onto Main Street. She'd been jogging for nearly half an hour when she neared the fire station again. She slowed to a walk, giving Bacchus a chance to cool down before they arrived back at her apartment.

As she passed the station, she glanced into the bay and her pulse sped up.

Chance stood with a barbell laden with what appeared to be some heavy weights at each end. He was shirtless, his upper body bathed in a sheen of perspiration, his muscles straining under the weight as he curled the bar up to his chest and back down.

Kate stumbled to a stop, her heart pounding, heat rushing through her body.

Holy hell, the man's bulging muscles made her want to reach out and lick the sweat off his skin.

Bacchus let out a woof, startling Kate back to her senses.

"Shush, Bacchus," she said and tried to drag him away from the front of the fire station.

He refused to budge, his attention on Chance as much as Kate's had been a second before.

She glanced toward Chance, praying he hadn't heard Bacchus or noticed the two of them standing there, staring at him.

Her gaze met his.

Damn. Too late. He'd seen them.

Once again, Kate tried to get Bacchus to come with her, by yanking on his lead, forgetting all the commands she'd learned that Bacchus knew.

"Good morning, Kate." Chance left the shadows of the bay and stepped out into the sunshine. His body glowed like a Greek god's, a god come down to grace mere mortals on Earth.

When she realized her mouth was hanging open, Kate snapped it shut and forced a cool smile to her lips. "Good morning."

Chance's brow dipped as he neared her. "I thought you started work today."

She nodded. "I do. At eight o'clock. That's another hour from now."

"That's right. I hope you slept well in the apartment last night."

"Like a baby," she lied. "And you?"

"Never better," he said.

If she wasn't mistaken, the dark circles under his eyes told a very different story. Her lips quirked upward at the corners. Had he had as lousy a night's sleep as she had? That would be just desserts, since he'd been the one to initiate that kiss.

How dare he start something when she'd specifically said she wasn't interested in a relationship? She should be angry with him. But she couldn't muster the ire when he stood there, naked from the waist up, making her insides tremble and warm.

"Bacchus appears to be adjusting well to his new environment," Chance said.

Kate glanced down at the dog, lying at her feet and panting. "He enjoyed the exercise and only tried to drag me off a couple of times when he saw a squirrel or another dog. I've been remiss keeping up on his discipline."

"I'm sure you'll have him squared away soon. In the meantime, he looks happy." Chance bent to scratch behind Bacchus's ears.

The dog leaned into his hand and licked his fingers. Then he rolled onto his back.

Chance chuckled and rubbed Bacchus's belly.

All the while Chance gave Bacchus his attention, Kate's was on Chance's shoulders, back and torso. The man was built like a weightlifter. Every time he moved, his muscles rippled and flexed.

Kate swallowed hard to keep from moaning and clenched her fists to refrain from reaching out to touch his tempting body. He was a beautiful specimen of a man. And she'd be smart to steer clear of him. Getting involved with the motorcycle-riding firefighter could only lead her to heartache. If she did decide to go after such a man, he would be her rebound man. She needed time between relationships. One weekend was not enough.

Although, if she looked at the reality of her association with Randy, it had ended the day she'd deployed. That had been over nine months ago. She'd been over him long before she'd returned to end it.

Still…she hadn't come to Hellfire to jump back into something she wasn't ready for. And she doubted seriously she'd ever be ready for a man like Chance Grayson. Her pulse pounded hard in her veins at the thought of being with the man.

He straightened, his bare chest rising up in front of her face.

Her tongue stuck to the roof of her suddenly dry mouth. "I'd better get going." *Before I drool.* "I have to get a shower and get dressed before I report for duty."

"I hope your first day goes well," he said.

"Bacchus, *fuss.*"

The dog jumped to his feet and stood beside Kate.

"Again, if you need a place to train Bacchus, you can always do it here. We have plenty of room. The guys might get a kick out of it, too. It can be pretty boring around here, if all is well in the county."

She smiled. "Thanks." Then she beat a hasty retreat before her knees gave out and she dissolved into a puddle of goo.

As she hurried away, she cursed herself beneath her breath. Why did she have such a reaction to the man? She'd stood there like the village idiot, her tongue practically lolling from her head, like Pavlov's dog salivating for his treat.

Back at her apartment, she stripped naked and stepped into the tiny bathroom. A cool shower helped set her mind straight and bring her body temperature back into the normal range. By the time she was dressed in her jeans and the sheriff's department T-shirt, she felt more in control and ready to face the day ahead.

CHAPTER 7

Anxious to start out on the right foot, Kate hefted her backpack over one shoulder and left her apartment twenty minutes before she had to be at work. The walk to the sheriff's office took less than five, so she arrived in plenty of time.

Sheriff Olson was inside talking with Nash Grayson when she entered the front reception area.

The sheriff turned to her and smiled. "Good morning, Deputy Bradley. Are you ready to start work for the department?"

She stood tall, her shoulders back and her chin held high. "Yes, sir." Excited to start this new chapter of her life, she eagerly awaited her orders.

"I'm pairing you with Deputy Grayson today. He'll train you on the vehicles, computers and equipment we use here. Then you'll do a ride along for the rest of the day to familiarize yourself with our area of responsibility. I've scheduled you to go to the basic law enforcement academy in two months. In the meantime, you can ride shotgun with Grayson and start training online to get a leg up on laws, crimes, crisis intervention and more. You can also get a start on training Bacchus for drug detection." He nodded toward Nash Grayson. "You'll be learning from one of the best men on my team. Now, I have a meeting to attend at Town Hall."

The sheriff left the building, and Kate smiled across at Nash. "I'm ready for whatever you have in store."

"Good, let's get some of the administrative stuff done." He walked her through the building to a room where one person sat in the middle of an array of monitors, a headset fitted over her head and a microphone curled around her cheek.

She smiled up at Kate and held out her hand. "Welcome to the department, I'm Ava Lovelady. I work 911 dispatch for the county."

"She's also our computer guru," Nash said. "She'll get you set up with your login and password to get into the computer and databases you'll need to do your training and your job."

An hour later, Kate's head whirled with all the information they'd dumped on her. Much of it was familiar to her from when she'd been an MP in the Army, before she'd changed specialties to become a dog handler. But a lot was more complex and would take time to learn.

"You're looking a little overwhelmed," Nash said as he joined her in front of the coffeemaker.

"I am, a little," she admitted.

"Then it's time to take you out for a ride around town. I'll show you the hot spots, and the places to look out for."

Four hours later, Kate felt as if she'd seen every inch of Hellfire and half the county. Some of it she recalled, the rest she'd have to revisit a couple of times to commit to memory.

Bacchus rode in the back of the SUV, content to get out when they got out and sleep the rest of the time.

Their shift close to over, Nash led her to the evidence safe and pulled out a canvas bag marked with an C.

"Cannabis?" Kate asked, excitement building inside. She'd hoped to start Bacchus's training as soon as hers began. She grinned and held out her hand.

Nash shook his head. "You have to sign for it, first."

She took the clipboard and pen from a hook on the wall, wrote her name in block letters and then signed in the signature block.

Nash handed her the bag. "I'd like to watch, if you don't mind."

"Please. I'm proud of Bacchus and love to show off what he can do." She glanced into the safe. "I don't suppose you have any bomb materials in there, do you? It's good to start with something familiar to remind him of his training."

"As a matter of fact, we do have some C4 we confiscated from some teenagers blowing up dumpsters. They stole it from a mining company." He reached into the safe and pulled out a small brick of inert C4. Without something to detonate it, it was harmless.

Again, Kate signed for the item before taking it. "I need to grab my backpack."

She hurried to where she'd stashed her backpack in the breakroom. She slung it over her shoulder and rejoined Nash in the hallway.

"We have a little room out behind the office to work in for a start. If you need more, we can go to the fire station."

"Let's start here," Kate said, a little too quickly. She'd have to have more room, eventually, but last night's kiss was still too fresh on her mind, and she needed to focus on Bacchus, not a handsome, barely dressed firefighter.

"Out back it is." Nash led the way. He paused before exiting through the back door. "Do you want me to go first and hide the items?"

Kate nodded. "Only the C4. I'll start familiarizing

Bacchus with the cannabis after we've played with the C4."

His eyebrows shot up. "Played?"

"To Bacchus, sniffing is a form of work and play. When he finds something he's supposed to find, I reward him with his toy."

"I thought dog handlers trained with treats."

"Some do. Bacchus is motivated by a chance to play with his Kong." She unzipped her backpack and held it open for Nash to see the toy inside.

Bacchus sat by her feet, looking up at her, his mouth open, his attention focused on her backpack.

Kate chuckled. "He knows I have it, and he's excited to get to work."

"Now, I'm excited to see him work." Nash took the C4 out the door. A moment later, he returned and grinned. "I hid it behind that stack of old tires."

"Good. I'll walk him around the perimeter and get there eventually. It's been a while, but he should remember how to seek." Kate gave Bacchus the German command to seek, let him have the length of his lead and followed him around the small area between the office building and the storage unit. Bacchus sniffed at a rolling trash container, a stack of paint buckets, empty pallets and, finally, the piled tires.

Bacchus sniffed once and laid on the ground, looking up at Kate with what appeared to be an expectant grin.

"Good dog," she said in a singsong voice. Kate reached into her backpack, pulled out the Kong and handed to Bacchus.

He gripped it in his teeth and dropped to the ground, his tail wagging.

Kate let him have a few moments with his toy before she gave him the command to release it. "*Aus!*"

He hesitated, but then spit out the toy and lay staring at it until Kate picked it up and replaced it in her backpack.

"Want me to hide it again?" Nash asked.

"No. He remembers well enough. I want to familiarize him with the cannabis." She pulled the bag of marijuana from her pocket end held it out to Bacchus.

He sniffed the bag and looked to her.

She gave him the command to sit. "*Sitz.*"

Bacchus sat back on his haunches, his tail wagging.

She handed him the Kong.

The dog played with the toy for a minute, and then they repeated the process.

After four times repeating the command to sit after sniffing the cannabis, Bacchus sniffed and automatically sat without being given the command.

"Good dog." Kate ruffled his neck and handed him the Kong. "It's about repetition and reward."

"I see that. He's smart to have picked up so quickly."

"It will take longer to fully entrench the scent."

"Why did he lay down when he sniffed the C4 but not the cannabis?"

"I trained him to lay down when he sniffed explosives. I wanted him to perform different functions for each task. Lay down for explosives, sit for marijuana."

"Okay. I hope he won't have to sniff for bombs any time soon."

"You and me both," Kate said. "*Aus.*"

Bacchus released the Kong and stood with his tail wagging, ready to play again.

Nash glanced at his watch. "We're officially off duty."

"I think that's enough for the day." Kate packed the Kong in her backpack. "Thank you for your patience with the new kid today."

"It was my pleasure. You'll have to get used to me being around. Until you go to the academy, we'll be partners."

"I'm honored," she said with a nod.

"And I look forward to learning more about Bacchus and training a working dog."

Together, they walked back to the office and entered through the back door.

"I hope my brother didn't do or say anything to offend you last night," Nash said.

Heat rushed up into Kate's cheeks. She ducked her head, pretending to look back at Bacchus to hide her blush. "I don't know what you're talking about."

"My family tends to come on a little strong when it comes to the happiness of one of our own. They can be overzealous in their matchmaking attempts."

She laughed. "They didn't bother me. I took it all in the spirit of a joke."

"If only Chance would. He tends to be touchy about the whole dating thing. He doesn't talk about his last deployment. But it might help you to know he lost someone he cared about in Afghanistan the last time he was there. He hasn't been the same since."

"I'm sorry to hear that. But he doesn't have to worry about me. I just got rid of one hundred-eighty pounds of dead weight in a lousy ex-boyfriend. I'm in no hurry to take on any other man in my life." She reached down and patted the dog's head. "Bacchus is the only guy in my life right now, and I mean to keep it that way for a while."

Nash nodded. "Understood. I just wanted you to know a little about what makes Chance so cantankerous sometimes. Don't take anything he says too personally. He used to be a fun-loving guy."

"Thanks for letting me know."

Nash stopped walking and turned toward her. "Do me a favor, will ya?"

"What's that?"

"Don't tell him I was talking about him. He'd skin me alive."

Kate held up her hand as if taking an oath. "I promise not to say a word to him." If she had it her way, she'd avoid him altogether. That haunted look in his eyes could melt even the hardest of hearts, if she let it.

CHANCE HAD SPENT the day working out, washing the truck and cleaning the fire station from top to bottom. After Nash drove by in his service vehicle with Kate in the passenger seat the first time, Chance found himself watching for them again and again. Every time a sheriff's department vehicle passed, his head jerked up and he stared hard at the passenger seat, lookin' for the pretty new deputy. At the end of the day, he sat in a chair inside the open bay. The weather had been so warm that the evening breeze helped to cool down the interior of the station to an almost tolerable temperature.

Daniel had kitchen duty that night, and volunteers had arrived for training after dinner.

"Dinner will be ready in thirty minutes," Becket called out. He'd come to the station for the training and would leave shortly after to return to the ranch and his lady love Kinsey. "Did you hear me?"

Chance nodded. "Heard you. Thanks."

About that time, Kate and Bacchus appeared,

walking from the sheriff's office back toward her apartment.

Before he could ask himself why, he sprang from his seat and hurried out to her.

Bacchus leaped forward and planted his paws on Chance's chest.

This time, Chance didn't fall backward over the curb. Instead, he ruffled the fur around Bacchus's neck.

"Bacchus, *fuss*," Kate said in a firm, commanding tone

Bacchus hesitated, his tail wagging. Then he dropped to all four paws and stared up at Chance.

"I'm so sorry," Kate said. "Bacchus appears to approve of you. I've never had him jump up on anyone else." She frowned down at the dog.

"I'll take it as a compliment," he said, brushing the dog hairs off his shirt. "Flannigan is making a massive amount of lasagna tonight. Would you care to join us? It's a full house at the station tonight with all of the volunteers here for annual CPR training."

She looked toward the station and back at him. "I think it would be better if I didn't."

"You wouldn't be the only female. We have a couple of women volunteers as well."

"I'm pretty tired after a full first day on the job." She gave him a hint of a smile. "But thanks."

Chance nodded. "Yeah, I get it. First days are

always tiring. If you change your mind, come anyway. Flannigan's lasagna is pretty good."

"Thanks." She stepped back. "Have a good evening."

"You, too," Chance said. "Oh, and don't forget, I still owe you a riding lesson."

She nodded. "I didn't forget. About that…"

"You don't have to commit now," he hurried to say, half expecting her say she didn't want to go through with the lesson. He stopped her before she could. "When we both have time, we can talk about it then."

She nodded. "Okay. Well, I'd better go." Kate turned and walked away, half-dragging Bacchus along behind her. The dog kept looking back as if he'd rather have stayed with Chance.

As soon as Kate was out of sight, Chance returned to his chair inside the bay, wondering what he was doing asking Kate to spend more time with him. Hadn't she made it clear that she didn't want anything to do with him, or any other man for that matter?

"Did she shoot you down?" Becket appeared beside him.

"No, she didn't shoot me down," Chance said. "Why does everyone assume I'm asking Kate out, and that she shoots me down? I just suggested she might want to join us for dinner since Flannigan's lasagna is so good."

Becket shook his head, his mouth twisting. "And she shot you down."

Chance flung his arm in the air. "Am I talking to a brick wall? She didn't shoot me down. If anything, she shot Flannigan's lasagna down. Maybe she doesn't like Italian food."

"Have you considered that she might be avoiding you?" Becket asked.

Chance had not only considered it, he was convinced that was why she'd refused to come to dinner at the station. If anyone else had asked and he wasn't going to be there, she probably would have agreed. He shouldn't have kissed her the night before. After telling her they could just be friends, he'd gone and ruined it by stepping out of the "friend zone" and into the gray and troubled area of potential lovers.

Becket clapped a hand on his back. "If you really like her, don't give up. Persistence can pay off." He chuckled. "Just don't go overboard and become a stalker."

"You're not helping, brother," Chance muttered.

"No?" Becket's eyebrows rose. "But am I irritating you?"

"Absolutely," Chance responded.

"Then my job here is done." He sniffed the air. "I believe there might be some garlic bread with my name on it. I'd better get in there before someone eats it all."

Chance sat outside for a while longer, not at all

anxious to join the others, who would be sure to rib him about being shot down again. Becket would no doubt spread the word. After all, what were brothers for but to torment each other?

Despite being shot down, Chance couldn't pass on Flannigan's Italian dinner. He entered the station with one last glance in the direction Kate had gone. Perhaps, he should have had someone who hadn't kissed her ask her to have dinner with them. She had to be hungry, and he bet she hadn't been to the store yet.

Great, so now his kiss had made him doubly guilty. Not only did he feel as though he'd cheated on Sandy's memory, but he'd also deprived Kate of a good meal, because she'd felt the need to avoid him and his unwanted kisses.

Hell, he was screwing up right and left. So much for getting his life on track. Who knew it would be this hard?

CHAPTER 8

KATE HURRIED TO HER APARTMENT, arriving in time to see a sleek white sedan pull into the driveway. A woman with bleached blond hair stepped out wearing a short white skirt, matching jacket and a gorgeous pair of three-inch high turquoise stilettoes. When she straightened, she stood as tall as Kate in her boots.

"You must be Kate," the woman said and glanced down at the dog beside her. "And this must be Bacchus."

"I am and he is," Kate said. "And you are?"

"Remiss in my introduction." She grinned and held out her hand. "I'm Lola Engel, your landlord." Her smile twisted. "Although, I feel downright guilty charging you rent when there's this nasty pile of rubble smelling up the place." Her smile flipped upside down. "It used to be such a lovely old house."

"I'm sorry for your loss."

"I'm just thankful my kitten and I made it out alive." She glanced up at the garage apartment. "The garage seems so lonely without a house next to it. Hopefully, that will soon change." She smiled at Kate. "I'm sorry I wasn't here to welcome you last night, but I see you found it. Is it all right for now?"

"It's fine," Kate said, instantly liking Lola and her incredibly tall high heels. "I left the windows open last night to air out the smoke smell."

"I'm sorry for that, but it will take time and maybe a coat of paint to tamp down that odor." She hooked Kate's arm. "Did you start work today?"

"I did," Kate said.

"Then I guess you met one of the Grayson brothers." She grinned. "Nash."

"I did." Kate smiled. "As a matter of fact, I met all of the Graysons last night. Nash invited me to have dinner with the family at their ranch."

Lola clapped her hands. "Aren't they a lovely family?"

Kate nodded. "Yes, they are." One in particular had a lovely kiss.

"Then you met Chance." Lola heaved a huge sigh. "I had the hots for that boy for so long."

Kate's heart fluttered at the mention of Chance. She schooled her expression to what she hoped was indifference. "You had the hots for Chance?"

Lola waved her hand. "I know. You're wondering

what an older woman like me would want with a younger man like Chance. Well, I might be in my late thirties—don't let anyone tell you differently—but I'm not dead. I have a fine appreciation for handsome men." Her smile spread wider across her face. "Only I was targeting the wrong one."

"What do you mean?"

"I went after Chance, when the man I fell in love with was a member of his crew, Daniel Flannigan." She leaned close to Kate. "Let me tell you, I taught that young man a few things about making love to a mature woman." She crossed her arms over her chest, her left hand on display with a ring shining brightly on her third finger. "We're getting married as soon as the house is built. Not a day sooner. I refused to live in his trailer or have him live with me in the back of my shop. I want to enjoy being together from the day we say I do."

Kate laughed. "I admire that you know what you want."

"And I'm not afraid to go after it." She hooked Kate's arm. "Now, my Daniel is cooking for the fire department tonight. We're going."

Kate shook her head. "I need to get ready for work tomorrow."

"I call bullshit." Lola winked. "Daniel is a good cook. One of the reasons I love him so much. But not the main one. Anyway, I want to surprise him by showing up a day earlier than he expects. Come with me so I don't have to walk in alone."

Kate opened her mouth to say she couldn't but didn't get the chance.

"I won't take no for an answer," Lola warned. She turned Kate toward her apartment. "Hurry, go change into something glamorous. I'll wait for you. And while you're getting ready, I can feed Bacchus." She marched Kate up the stairs and into her apartment.

Short of being rude, Kate really had no other choice but to do as her landlord demanded. She changed into a denim skirt and a white sleeveless knit shirt that hugged her breasts and accentuated her narrow waist. When she slipped her feet into a pair of flat sandals, Lola looked at her in horror.

"Oh, sweetie, tell me you have a pair of heels." She stood staring at the flat sandals, her face creased in a frown.

"I do have a pair, but this is a denim skirt. Aren't casual sandals what goes with denim?"

"Honey, when you have a choice between flats and heels, go with heels every time. Unless you're hiking through the woods, of course. Heels make you look taller and tighten your calves to perfection."

Kate grimaced. "I'm not that comfortable wearing heels, but if you think it's the right thing to wear…" She reached into the bottom of the wardrobe and extracted her one pair of high heeled sandals with narrow silver straps that crisscrossed over the top of her feet. She slipped her feet into them and almost groaned.

"Those will do for now. Sometime soon, you need to come to my shop, and I'll find the perfect pair and fit for you. You can have stylish shoes without completely sacrificing comfort, I promise. Do you have a brush?"

Kate handed her a brush.

"Turn around," Lola commanded.

Kate turned and let Lola pull out the elastic band holding back her hair. In quick, strong strokes, she brushed the tangles out of Kate's hair.

"There." Lola stood back and smiled. "A dab of lipstick, and you'll do."

Kate touched her lips with her only tube of rose-colored lipstick and turned. "Better?"

"Perfect. Now, let's go before they run out of food. I'm starving, and I can't wait to see my man." Lola led the way out of the apartment and down the stairs.

Kate held her breath as the other woman navigated the staircase in her three-inch heels. "I don't know how you do it," she muttered as she held onto the rail and eased herself down the steps on her two-inch silver sandals. "There's a reason I don't wear heels."

"Honey, you look fabulous. That's enough reason to wear heels." Lola winked.

When Kate made it to the bottom, Lola offered

her arm. "Let's go get some dinner and a whole lot of lovin'."

"I'll stick with dinner. The lovin' part I'll leave to those who are better at it."

Lola shot her a narrowed glance. "I take it you've been unlucky in that direction?"

"And how." Kate held onto Lola's arm as they walked the two blocks to the fire station. She gave her the digest version of how she'd found her boyfriend in bed with another woman in the apartment Kate had been paying rent on during her deployment.

Lola winced. "Ouch. That was harsh. I hope you booted his ass out."

"I did. And moved here the same day."

"A fresh start is always good." Lola's eyebrows dipped. "He won't try to get you back, will he?"

"I doubt that. I had the police there to see him to the door. Unfortunately for him, he dropped a bag of cocaine in front of them. He ended up in jail. I doubt seriously he'll want to have anything more to do with me."

Lola laughed. "Sounds like he deserved the jail time."

"I doubt they'll keep him long. Possession isn't as tough a sentence as distribution."

"Still, he deserved to be thrown in the slammer. Anyone who'd use one of our members of the armed services while they're deployed and can't do a thing about it, should be stripped naked, tarred and feathered and marched down Main Street for all to see what a jerk he was. Jail time is too easy on the bastard."

"Lola Engel, I like the way you think." She squeezed the woman's arm and grinned. And that's how they arrived at the fire station.

CHANCE SAT at the back of the station at one of the tables they'd pulled out for the dinner and training. He held a red stadium cup of iced tea in his hand, wishing it was a beer. While everyone around him was laughing and joking, he sank into that dark place he'd inhabited all too often since he'd returned from the war.

"Hey, Chance." Becket pulled up a chair across from him and laid his plate full of Italian deliciousness in front of him. "You better hurry and get yours before it's all gone."

"Don't bother. I got a plate for you." Rider set two plates filled with lasagna and garlic breadsticks on the table, one in front of Chance, the other in front of an empty chair he quickly plunked himself into.

"Thanks," Chance said. "I wasn't all that hungry."

"Well, if you're not eating it, I will." Rider started to take the plate back.

Chance gripped the edge and held on to it. The rich tomato-y scent of lasagna made his mouth

118

water, and his stomach reminded him that it needed to be fed. "I said I wasn't. But I am now."

Becket chuckled and dug into his food. "Flannigan knows his pasta."

"What's got you down in the dumps?" Rider asked and took a bite of a garlic breadstick.

Chance frowned. "Who said I'm down in the dumps?"

"Seriously, dude," Rider said. "You'd have to be blind to miss that look of abject misery on your face."

His frown deepening, Chance cut into the lasagna. "I'm not miserable."

"You could have fooled us." Daniel brought a plate of food and sat across from Rider. "That's the same face I have when Lola's out of town. You really are taking it hard that the pretty deputy shot you down, aren't you?"

Chance slammed his fork onto the table so hard everyone standing nearby stopped talking and turned to see what the commotion was about.

Heat stole into his cheeks, and he picked up his fork. "Dropped it." To prove everything was all right, he scooped up a chunk of the steaming hot lasagna and shoved it into his mouth. And promptly burned his tongue. Forcing a smile to his face, he turned to Daniel and swallowed. "She didn't shoot me down, nor did she have a reason to shoot me down. I'm not interested. She's not interested. The end." He stared pointedly around the table at his friend and two brothers. "Understood?"

Becket held up his hands. "Whatever you say. I'll stay out of it."

"I guess you don't care that your little deputy just walked into the station with Lola then, do you?" Rider asked with a twisted grin.

Chance spun toward the open bay doors just in time to see Kate, Bacchus and Lola step out of the sunlight into the shaded bay. Immediately, they were surrounded by the men waiting their turn in line for the lasagna.

"Yeah. Not interested, my ass," Rider mumbled and shoved a breadstick into his mouth.

"Shut up, Rider," Chance said through gritted teeth. He fought the urge to jump up from his seat and cross the floor to break up the gang gathered around Kate and Lola. If he truly wasn't interested, he wouldn't be itching to get up and go see what had made Kate change her mind about joining them for dinner.

"This must be my lucky day." Daniel pushed back from the table. "If you'll excuse me, I need to go kiss my girl." He left Chance and his brothers to cross the floor and wade through the men circled around the women.

Chance found himself envying Daniel and his openness about loving and dating Lola. Not that Chance was interested in loving or dating Kate. But for some crazy reason, he wasn't keen on the idea of her loving or dating anyone else.

"If looks could kill, every one of those guys standing near Kate would be lying on the ground, twitching in death throes," Becket commented. "Why are you so adamant that you're not interested in Kate? You clearly are. Why deny it?"

"Will you leave it?" Chance said and dropped his gaze to his plate, pretending to enjoy the food Daniel had spent so much time putting together for the training event that evening. He told himself it didn't matter if a hundred guys flirted with Kate. She wasn't his girl, and she didn't want to be. So, why was he clenching his fists and gnashing his teeth?

"I'm going to go rescue her from the guys," Becket said. "Lola just ditched her for Daniel." He pushed to his feet.

Chance stood so fast, his chair tipped over backward and landed with a loud clatter against the concrete floor. He stood the chair on its feet then busted through the men around Kate. "Change your mind?" he asked Kate, holding out his arm.

She gladly took it and grimaced. "Lola made me come." Her gaze went to the woman and the night's chef where they were locked in each other's arms, kissing.

"I'd tell them to get a room, but they don't need to be told," Chance shook his head. "They will soon enough."

Kate laughed, the sound beautiful and heartfelt. It hit him like a sucker-punch to the gut and made him want to make her do it again. "Hungry?" he asked.

"Very," she said, rubbing a hand against her belly. "I wasn't looking forward to opening a can of soup. I could stand some real food."

"Fortunately, we only serve real food at the station," he said. "And by real food, I mean steak, chicken, potatoes and stuff that sticks to a man's ribs and fuels him with the energy he needs in case he has to fight a fire."

"Sounds positively healthy," she declared.

"Don't believe it for a moment. We all have our ideas about what's best for us. Jace Kelly would have pizza every night of the week, if he could."

"Hey, I heard that," Jace said from across room. "And what's wrong with pizza? It has meat and cheese. That's protein, isn't it?"

"And a whole lot of calories." Becket joined Chance. He held out his hand to Kate. "How are you after your first day on the job with the sheriff's department?"

"Good," she said, shaking it firmly.

Chance frowned at Becket's easy familiarity with Kate.

Becket turned to Chance. "Aren't you going to offer to get her a plate of Flannigan's finest?"

Heat rose up Chance's neck. "I was getting to it

when you interrupted." He held out a hand. "Come with me. Dan always leaves a tray full of lasagna warming in the oven while the others are being devoured."

Kate hesitated for a moment, and then put her hand in his. "Lead the way before I pass out from starvation."

"Can't have that, now can we?" His mood lighter than it had been in a long time, Chance led her and Bacchus into the kitchen where Daniel had left one tray of his spicy Italian meal in the oven just like Chance had said.

Grabbing an oven mitt, he pulled out the tray and set it on a brass trivet in the shape of a firefighter's hat. Then he pulled a real plate out of the cabinet, not the paper ones they were using out in the bay, and a spatula out of the drawer.

"You don't have to wait on me. I'm capable of helping myself," she reminded him.

"You're new around here. I'm just trying to be nice." He scooped a heaping helping onto the plate and handed her a fork. "We can eat in here to avoid the crowd outside, if you like."

"Thanks." She took the plate to the table and slid into a chair. "It's been a long day."

Chance put a smaller piece of the lasagna on another plate and joined her at the table.

She stared at her heaping plate and his smaller one. "Is that all you're having?"

He nodded. "I had some already. This would be seconds."

"Okay, then. I was beginning to feel like a glutton." She dug her fork into the tomato-y, cheesy pasta. "Because I'm hungry enough to eat every last bite."

"It's good to see a woman who doesn't pick at her food."

"Oh, right, you say that now," she said between bites. "But if a woman gets fat, you'd be singing a different tune."

"I've seen you out jogging. I'd struggle to keep up with you. I'm sure you burn off every last calorie you consume."

She shrugged. "For the most part."

"Oh, wait." Chance jumped up and pulled another tray from the warming oven. This one was filled with garlic breadsticks. "You can't have Italian pasta without garlic bread." He placed a basket full of bread in front of her.

"Mmm." She took one of the breadsticks and bit off the end. After she'd eaten the last bite of her lasagna and the breadstick, she leaned back and rested a hand over her flat belly. "That beat the hell out of a can of soup and a peanut butter and jelly sandwich. I'll have to jog a couple of extra miles to burn that off."

"I've been meaning to get back to jogging on pavement. Mind if I join you on my days off?"

"You mean you'd rather jog than sleep?" she asked.

"I need incentive." Which wasn't a lie. "I usually come in and jog on the treadmill. But you and I both know it's different than jogging on pavement."

Kate nodded. "I get out there around six-thirty. It gives me enough time to get thirty minutes in before I have to shower and get to the office by eight."

"I can be there," Chance promised.

"All the way from the ranch?"

He nodded. "I have an alarm."

She raised and lowered a shoulder. "When will you start?"

"How's tomorrow morning? I have the next two days off, and I don't report to work until seven in the morning the following day."

Kate's brow wrinkled.

"Don't worry. I just need to get out. I promise not to bug you. I know you're not into relationships, and neither am I. I see it as a chance to throw everyone off. If my family thinks I'm seeing you, they'll get off my back about dating."

Kate's lips spread into a grin. "And if the rest of the people in town think you and I are dating, maybe they'll leave me alone as well."

"Right. Win-win either way you look at it," Chance said. "Do we have a deal?"

With a nod, Kate held out her hand. "We have a deal."

"Friends?" he said as he shook her hand.

"Friends," she repeated.

"Then tomorrow, we'll show Hellfire that we're together, even though we both know we're not." Chance grinned. "I don't know why I didn't think of that before. It's the perfect solution to meddling family members." He sat back in his chair. "So, what are you doing with the rest of your evening?"

"Going home, taking a shower and curling up in bed with a good book." She smiled. "I probably won't even make it through a chapter before I fall asleep."

An image of Kate curled up in bed reading a book flashed through Chance's mind and made his groin tighten. He shifted in his seat to relieve the pressure. "I'd offer to bring a movie over, but I'm on duty tonight."

"No worries. I really am tired." She pushed back from the table and stood, teetering a little in her heels.

"By the way, you look great," Chance said. "But aren't those hard to walk in?"

Kate laughed. "They weren't my idea."

Chance chuckled. "Let me guess…Lola."

She nodded. "I like her. A lot."

"She's a little eccentric, but Daniel is crazy about her. She lost her husband a few years back and wasn't looking for a replacement."

"What was it your sister Lily said?" Kate tapped a finger to her chin. "You seem to find what you're looking for, when you aren't looking."

Chance nodded. "Sometimes my sister shows a lot more maturity than her years."

"I'd better go."

"Right. I'll walk you to the door." He cupped her elbow in his hand and led her through the kitchen, down a hallway and out through the open bay where the others were just finishing up dinner and clearing the tables for the training.

Lola joined Kate. "I'll walk with you. I have to get my car and go to the shop. I'm exhausted." She smiled at Chance. "I hope you all have a quiet night."

"Thanks." Chance stood at the corner of the building until Lola and Kate disappeared down Main Street.

A large hand clapped him on the back. "She's pretty and smart," Becket said.

"Yes, she is. But I'm not looking for anything more than a running buddy."

"Since when have you gotten back into running?" Becket asked.

"Since a certain deputy joined the sheriff's department," Rider answered, joining the brothers.

Chance flung his hands in the air. "Are we really going there again? Come on, we have work to do tonight. Then I'm going to try to catch some Zs."

"So, you can run after the new deputy tomorrow?" Rider laughed and held up his hands. "Okay, I'll lay off. Let's get this training started. I have a date with Salina on video chat later tonight."

"When will she be finished with PA school?"

"Not soon enough," Rider said, grimacing. "I look forward to having her home full time, not just on breaks between semesters."

They were almost through training when a call came through dispatch.

Daniel came out to the bay, slipping his arms through the sleeves of his turnout coat. "Got a dumpster fire. The teens are at it again. Let's roll."

Chance ran to get into his boots, pants and coat and grabbed his helmet.

Soon, they were pulling out of the station, lights flashing and sirens blaring.

A dumpster fire helped break the monotony of everyday life at the station. Hopefully, it ended at the dumpster and didn't spread to other buildings. Chance didn't want any lives to be at stake or more property damaged. He wanted to get to sleep early enough to be worth a damn jogging with Kate early in the morning.

CHAPTER 9

KATE FELL into a nice routine through the week of running with Chance in the morning and spending the day at the sheriff's department, training with Nash and retraining Bacchus to sniff for drugs.

She looked forward to the morning jogs with Chance. They talked a little the first day, learning more about each other.

He'd grown up in Hellfire, living on the family ranch. He liked pepperoni pizza and riding horses. His favorite seasons were spring and fall. He was easily frustrated with his siblings, but would take a bullet for any one of them. And he missed being a part of the military, but was glad to be home.

The more she learned about Chance, the more she realized what a jerk Randy had been. He'd had no ambition, no manners and no loyalty to anyone but himself. Had Kate known there were real men out there like Chance, she never would have looked twice at Randy.

She chalked up her mistake to loneliness and having no one else in her life at the time. Randy had been nice to her, at first, and Kate had been needy enough to fall for his lies.

But Kate had come a long way from being that needy for attention and love. In Afghanistan, she'd learned she was worth a whole lot more than what Randy had to offer. She learned to like her own company and not feel lonely when she was alone.

On the third morning, they slowed on their way back into Hellfire and walked the few blocks to the station to cool down.

"I still owe you a riding lesson," Chance said.

"I'd like that," Kate said. "I've enjoyed our running in the morning. Thanks."

"No, thank you. It gets me out of the station and off the treadmill. I like having someone to run with as well."

"It's nice to have a friend in town." Kate shot Chance a smile.

Chance smiled back. "It's nice that you call me a friend."

Kate frowned. "Look, Chance, I don't want to cramp your style. If you find someone you want to date, just let me know. It could be awkward if you're still running with me."

Chance's lips pressed into a thin line. "I'm not planning on dating anyone anytime soon."

She cast a sideways glance his way. "Someone burn you in the past? I know all about being burned."

He walked on for a few moments before answering. "No, not burned. Someone I cared about died in my arms."

Kate reached out to touch Chance's arm, bringing him to a halt. "Oh, Chance. I'm so sorry. That had to hurt deeply."

He nodded. "The bullet was meant for me. Only Sandy caught it."

"While you were in Afghanistan?" Kate asked softly.

He nodded and resumed walking. "It's been two years. You'd think the memories would have faded by now."

"Something like that might take a lot longer." And now, Kate knew the reason why Chance didn't want a relationship. "She must have been special."

Again, he nodded. "She was."

Sadness sank deep in Kate's belly. How could she compete with a ghost? Not that she was in a competition. But if she was, she would never win. Chance's Sandy had been the one for him. In her death, she'd died perfect. Nothing Kate, or any other woman, could do would ever measure up.

As they approached the fire station, Kate looked ahead. "Will I see you in the morning?"

"No, I'm on duty tomorrow through your running time. The weekend is coming up. Are you off on Saturday? We could do that riding lesson then."

"About that lesson… We don't have to. I'd understand if you're too busy. I'm still trying to get settled in, and Bacchus is finally ready to move on to another drug to sniff. I might be working the weekend on cocaine."

Chance chuckled. "That just sounds weird."

Kate smiled, glad the conversation had shifted to a lighter topic. "Bacchus picked up quickly with the marijuana. Sheriff Olson has a sample of cocaine I'll start training with this afternoon."

"I'm still going to take you out riding. If Saturday is good for you, I'd like to take you then. Bring your cocaine, and you can train Bacchus at the ranch. There should be lots of good places to hide drugs out there."

Kate laughed. "If anyone else heard us talking, they'd think we were drug runners."

He grinned. "So, Saturday?"

"Saturday," Kate agreed. "But if you get a better offer, my feelings won't be hurt if you call and cancel."

"Fair enough. But I can't think of a better offer than taking my new friend out for a ride." He touched his fingers to his temple in a mock salute. "Have a great day training with my brother."

"Will do. And don't get into any bad fires."

"It'll be another slow day in the neighborhood," Chance promised.

Kate hoped so. She hated to think of him running into a burning building. How did wives of firefighters remain calm when their men were on duty?

Not that Chance was her man, nor she his wife. But he was her friend, and she worried about him.

After a quick shower and a change into the uniform that had finally arrived the day before, she walked with Bacchus to the sheriff's office and started her day's training with Nash. They spent the early part of the day riding out in the countryside, where she learned about all the different roads leading into the Hill Country, both paved and unpaved. When they came back for lunch, Nash was tasked with transporting a prisoner from the county jail to the county courthouse for trial. They left the courthouse that afternoon and dropped the prisoner off at the jail. On their way back into the sheriff's office, the town of Hellfire was rocked with an earth-shaking explosion.

"What the hell?" Kate swayed for a moment, and then spun toward the sound.

A plume of smoke rose above the southeast corner of Hellfire.

"Come on. Let's go check it out." Nash ran back toward the SUV.

Kate held the back door for Bacchus to get in. She

jumped into the passenger seat and slammed the door as Nash shifted into reverse.

Lights flashing and sirens blaring, they followed the smoke to the southeast.

As they passed the fire station, men were leaping onto the big red truck as it edged out of the bay.

Kate thought she caught a glimpse of Chance climbing aboard but wasn't sure. When the men were dressed in their turn-out gear, they all looked alike— bulky and dull yellow with stripes of reflective tape across their arms and backs.

The SUV's radio crackled with the report of an explosion and fire on Poplar Street.

Nash responded that they were on their way. Another deputy checked in that he was on his way with a five-minute ETA.

Nash and Kate were the first of the first responders at the scene.

In a dingier side of the little town, where the buildings were showing their wear and not being maintained as well, someone had blown up a huge bin full of trash next to a wood-framed abandoned warehouse. The explosion had knocked a hole in the side of the building and set off a fire that was quickly consuming the old timbers and siding, eating into the walls and roof so quickly, the fire department would be hard-pressed to save the structure.

Sirens wailed as the fire engine whipped around the corner and came to a stop near the site.

Firefighters leaped from the truck and yanked the hoses loose, dragging them to the nearest hydrant.

People from the nearby neighborhood of shanty houses and run-down apartments gathered nearby.

Kate, Bacchus and Nash left the SUV and hurried to urge them to stay back and out of the way of the firefighters.

"Pay attention to the onlookers," Nash said in a hushed tone. "Sometimes the perpetrators like to watch the show."

As she spoke with bystanders, Kate studied them. Some were older men and women from nearby houses, concerned for their homes and neighbors.

A man stumbled out of the old warehouse, his clothes tattered, looking as if he hadn't had a bath in weeks. He carried an equally tattered duffel bag and a ragged sleeping bag slung over his shoulder. Staggering toward the firefighters, he shouted, "There are more people inside."

The firefighters ran into the burning building.

Kate could barely breathe as she waited for them to come back out.

Bacchus tugged at the end of his lead, sniffing the side of the building adjacent to the one on fire. He pulled her forward, eager to sniff more.

Kate eased forward, letting him continue his investigation while she watched for the firefighters, praying Chance wasn't one of them, but knowing in her heart he was.

Nash had hurried forward to get the homeless man out of the way of the men working the fire.

When Bacchus's lead suddenly went slack, she glanced down at him.

He lay on the ground, looking up at her.

Kate frowned. "What's wrong, Bacchus?"

He turned to sniff at a concrete block leaning against the wall of the building and turned back to her, his tail wagging as if he was waiting for her to give him his toy.

Kate's heart leaped into her throat. She backed away from the concrete block, dragging Bacchus away with her. "Nash!" Looking around desperately, she yelled again, "Nash!"

Deputy Grayson appeared at her side. "What's wrong?"

She pointed toward the concrete block leaning against the building adjacent to the one with the flames climbing higher into the sky. "Bacchus indicated he found something behind that concrete block."

Nash frowned. "Found what?"

Her blood running cold in her veins despite the heat of the blaze, Kate hurried to explain. "He laid down."

"I don't know what that means."

"It means he found explosives. I trained him to sit when he finds drugs." She looked around at the people standing nearby and the firefighters rushing out of the burning building, carrying or assisting a ragtag group of men from the smoke and destruction. "We have to get everyone back. Now."

Nash didn't need further direction. He spoke into the radio on his shoulder, warning dispatch and the other deputy who'd arrived at the scene of the potential of another explosion.

"I'll tell the firefighters," Kate said and ran toward the men gathered near the front of the burning building.

"Get these people out of here," she yelled as she ran forward. "You have to get out of here now!"

A firefighter stepped in front of her. "Kate, what's going on?" Chance gripped her shoulders and stared at her with a soot-covered face.

"Explosives. Bacchus indicated explosives against the side of the next building. Everyone needs to get back."

"Go. Take Bacchus and help get the bystanders back further. We'll take care of the rest."

She grabbed hold of his jacket, her heart pounding hard inside her chest. "You have to leave before the next one goes off."

"We will. But you need to go first. I can't do my job until you get out of the way."

She nodded and stepped back. Then she turned and ran toward the thickening crowd. "Move back!" She yelled. "Way back. There are more explosives. If you don't leave now, you'll be hurt."

The onlookers turned and walked or ran as fast as they could.

The homeless man who'd originally exited the burning building staggered toward the flames. "Rudy. Did you get Rudy out of there?"

Kate hurried toward him. "Sir, you have to leave this area now. There's a chance of another explosion happening. You're not safe here."

"But I can't find Rudy."

Her chest tightening, Kate looked around. "Who's Rudy?"

"My dog. He's still inside that building." He pushed past Kate and lumbered toward the building engulfed in flames.

Kate grabbed his arm and yanked him around. "You can't go in there. You have to leave this area immediately."

"I won't go without Rudy."

A firefighter emerged from the burning building, carrying a short-haired dog that appeared to be a cross between a Labrador retriever and a hound. As soon as he cleared the door, the dog wriggled out of the firefighter's arms and ran toward the homeless man beside Kate.

The man bent and caught the dog as he leaped into his arms. "Rudy. I thought you were a goner." He hugged the dog tightly, tears streaming down his cheeks making tracks through the grime.

"Now, go!" Kate turned the man around and gave him a gentle shove. "Hurry!"

Once the man was moving in the right direction, Kate started to turn around.

A man wearing a helmet and a fire-resistant uniform ran toward her. "Kate, get out of here!"

The moment she realized it was Chance, an explosion rocked the air and threw her to the ground.

Chance landed on top of her, covering her with his body. Pieces of brick, boards and glass blasted out from the point of detonation, raining down on them.

Something pierced the leg of Kate's uniform trouser and pinched her arm. Her ears rang from the concussion, and for a long moment, she couldn't catch her breath.

"Kate?" Chance lifted his head. "Are you okay?" He leaned up on his elbows and stared down into her face, his gaze sweeping over her features. "Talk to me, Kate."

"Can't…breathe…" she whispered.

Chance immediately rolled to the side.

As soon as he did, smoky air filled her lungs. She coughed and sat up, her head spinning. "Bacchus," she cried out.

The Malinois dropped down beside her and nuzzled her hand.

She pulled the animal into her arms and ran her hands over his body, feeling for wounds. She stopped when her fingers encountered the warm, wet stickiness of blood. "He's injured." Kate pushed to her knees and stared down at Bacchus.

"He's not injured, Kate," Chance said. "You are. That's your blood."

She stared at her forearm where a jagged scrape was bleeding onto the dog and laughed. The sound came out a little manic and relieved at the same time. "Oh, it's just me."

She sat back on her heels and looked around. "There could be more explosives."

"I doubt it. But it wouldn't hurt to get you out of here and let Bones check you out."

He helped her to her feet. When she wobbled, her head spinning a little, he bent and scooped her up in his arms.

"Hey, I can walk," she said, but didn't struggle. She liked how strong he was and how he made her feel cared for and protected. "What about the others? Someone might have real injuries."

"They're okay. You're the one bleeding."

"I am, aren't I?" she said, staring at her arm, dripping blood onto his jacket. "I'm sorry. I'm messing up your suit."

Chance shook his head. "You're killing me."

"Bacchus and I were only trying to help."

The dog trotting along beside them looked up.

"And thank goodness you were there to find those

explosives. It could have been bad if we hadn't gotten as far away as we did."

He took her to the other side of the fire truck where the EMT, Bones, was checking out the firefighters and the homeless men who'd been in the burning building.

An ambulance had just pulled up, and more emergency medical technicians jumped out and off-loaded a gurney.

Chance set her on her feet near Bones. Bacchus sat, his tail wagging, seeming to take it all in.

"Did you notice?" Kate said.

"Notice what?"

"Bacchus didn't run off after the explosion."

"That's good, right?"

"Yes. Maybe he's getting over his fear of things that go bang."

"Maybe." Chance interrupted Bones tending a cut on one of the firefighter's cheeks. "I need some of your medical supplies."

Bones moved aside so Chance could reach the kit. He glanced over at Kate. "I heard Bacchus saved us all."

Kate patted the dog's head, leaving a trail of blood. "He's a good dog."

Bones slapped an adhesive bandage onto Daniel's cheek. "You're good to go." Then he turned to Kate. "Here, let me."

Chance handed Bones what he needed to clean

ELLE JAMES

and wrap the wound. "You'll need to rewrap it once you've had a shower, but this will do for now."

She looked down at the bandage and smiled up at Chance and Bones. "Thanks, but I seem to have torn my new uniform as well." She held out her leg where the bottom of the pant leg was thick with her blood.

"Damn, why didn't you say anything?" Chance bent and ripped her trouser up to her knee.

"Hey. That's my new uniform."

"It was torn anyway, and the sheriff isn't going to give you a hard time about it," Nash said. "Are you?"

Sheriff Olson stepped up beside Kate. "I have another set due in the office tomorrow. Don't worry about it. You and Bacchus did good today."

"But the buildings..." She stared at the two buildings that were still burning. "They're a complete loss."

"Yeah, but they're just buildings. They can be replaced," the sheriff said. "Our men and women in uniform can't be."

Chance wrapped her leg in a swath of bandages. "The wound isn't that deep, so you won't need stitches, but this was all we had left. We have more supplies at the station, or we can swing by the clinic for some on the way through town."

"I'll be fine." Kate pushed to her feet. "See?" She was proud of herself for not even swaying when her head swam.

"Yeah. Come on, let's get you home," Nash said.

She shook her head. "There's still more work to do. You need to be here as well."

"But you've been injured," Chance argued.

"And if it was Nash, instead of me? Would you be as quick to send him home?"

"Yes," Chance said.

Kate raised her eyebrows and turned to Nash. "Would he?"

Nash shook his head. "He'd tell me to 'buck up, buttercup'."

Kate crossed her arms over her chest. "I'm staying. We can't have anyone interfering with the work you guys are doing to keep the fire from spreading." She pointed to Chance. "You have your job, go to it. And I'll do mine."

Chance frowned.

Sheriff Olson chuckled. "She's got spunk." He clapped his hands together. "Come on, let's get this place cleaned up."

Kate gathered Bacchus's lead. "I'm going to take Bacchus around the exterior of the surrounding buildings."

"Sounds like a good idea," the sheriff said. "I'll go with you. I'd like to see Bacchus in action."

For the next hour, Kate, Bacchus and the sheriff worked their way around the buildings in the area. Thankfully, no other explosives were detected. By the time they returned to the fire truck, the flames had been extinguished, and the men were returning the equipment to the truck.

Chance and Nash joined her and the sheriff.

"You want to ride back with me, or would you like to ride in the fire truck for a change?" Nash asked.

"I can ride in the truck?" Kate glanced up at the impressively large vehicle.

"You sure can." Chance helped her and Bacchus up into the seat and slid in next to them. Daniel Flannigan got into the driver's seat and glanced her way. "Ready?"

"Ready," she said.

Kate had been in big trucks before, having ridden in a variety of Army vehicles, but never in a bright red fire engine with a couple of hot firefighters on either side.

Her leg ached, and her arm stung, but she couldn't keep from grinning as she rode through the streets of Hellfire, like a kid on her favorite amusement ride.

When they reached the fire station, Chance was the first down. Bacchus leaped to the ground beside him. Then Chance grabbed Kate around the waist and guided her gently out of the vehicle.

Kate rested her hands on his shoulders to steady herself, laughing as she landed. "That was amazing."

He smiled into her eyes, his face close enough she could easily have moved closer and kissed him.

His gaze dropped to her lips, and he leaned closer.

"We'll take care of the truck, if you want to see Kate home," Daniel called out.

Chance's head jerked up, and the moment was gone. "Let me get out of this suit, and I'll see you home," he said, his voice gruff.

Kate backed away, letting her hands fall to her sides. The day had been hard, but worth every second —and she'd almost kissed a firefighter.

And she might have read too much into his look, but she could've sworn he'd almost kissed her.

CHAPTER 10

CHANCE HURRIED to shed his protective suit and scrub the soot off his hands and face. In less than two minutes, he returned to where Kate and Bacchus stood next to Daniel as he explained some of the features of the truck.

As he stopped beside her, he smiled. "I'm still on duty, but I can cut out for a few minutes to take you to your apartment in my truck."

"What if they get another call?" Kate asked.

"I have my radio. I can be back before they pull the truck out of the bay." He held up the radio, and then clipped it to his belt.

"I can walk home," she insisted.

"I'd rather take you." Chance hooked her elbow and led her toward his truck. "You lost a lot of blood."

"I didn't know you had a truck. I thought you rode a motorcycle."

He smiled. "I have both. It just so happened I couldn't get the bike started this morning, so I drove the truck."

"Well, darn. Next time, I'd like a ride on the bike."

"You're on—but after the riding lesson on the horse."

"Deal."

He helped her into the truck, careful of her injuries, and then climbed into the driver's seat.

"You were amazing today," Kate said.

Chance chuckled. "I was about to say the same thing about you."

All too soon, he pulled into the driveway in front of Lola's garage apartment.

"You don't have to walk me up. I know you have to get back to the station, and it's still light outside."

The sun was well on its way to the horizon, and the shadows were lengthening, but it remained light outside as Texas was prone to with its clear blue skies.

"Humor me, please. When I bring a woman home, I like to make sure she makes it safely into her place."

"I'd argue, but then you'd just take longer to get back to the station." She unbuckled her seatbelt.

"Let me get your door."

"Again, I'll refrain from argument. Anything to get you back to work before the entire town burns to the ground," she teased.

"What are the chances of another fire in Hellfire tonight?"

"I don't know. How often do you have people blowing up buildings?"

Chance rounded the front of the truck and opened her door. "You have me on that one. I can't remember the last time anything blew up in Hellfire." He held out his hand and helped Kate to the ground.

She winced when she put weight on her injured leg.

"Still hurting?" he asked, frowning down at her leg.

"Just got stiff." She smiled up at him, even if the smile appeared a little strained. "I'll be fine once I've had a shower and I'm in my PJs."

"You want me to stick around to apply a fresh dressing?"

She shook her head. "You're on duty. No. I can do it myself. You need to get back to the station."

"I can have someone else take my shift. All I have to do is call Big Mike. He'd fill in for me in a heartbeat. I've picked up his slack many times."

Kate touched Chance's arm, sending electric pulses through his entire body. "No. But thanks. It's nice to know someone is looking out for me."

"That's what friends are for."

She nodded. "I'm glad we're friends."

He wished they were so much more. The thought shocked him to his very core. How could he forget what he'd had with Sandy? But the thing was that Kate was there, alive, beautiful and real. She wasn't a ghost or a memory. She could be the key to Chance getting on with his life.

If he let her.

If she let him.

One step at a time, he reminded himself.

And he took the stairs up to her apartment one step at a time.

"Keys?" he said, holding out his hand.

"I've got this," she said and started toward the door with the key held out in front of her.

Before she could stick the key in the lock, Chance grabbed her hand, his heart stopping for a split second, his breath catching in his throat. "Wait."

Kate frowned. "Why?"

Chance touched the door with the tip of his finger, and it swung open. The door frame was splintered.

"Stay back," he said.

"I'm the deputy. You stay back," Kate said and pulled the weapon from the holster on her belt. Standing to the side of the door, she then nudged the door wider and peeked around the corner into the apartment. "Sweet Jesus," she whispered.

Chance and Bacchus pushed past her and charged inside.

"Hey, you could get killed that way," Kate said,

following him into what could only be described as a disaster.

Every drawer had been pulled out of the dresser and wardrobe. All of her clothes had been slung across the floor. The bed had been flipped and the mattress ripped, as if someone had taken a knife to the fabric and dragged it from one end to the other. The pillows had been shredded, and the carpet had been pulled up. Chance entered the bathroom where the shower curtain had been torn down, rod and all, and the lid to the toilet tank had been thrown into the bathtub where it had been broken.

"Are you sure another stick of dynamite didn't go off in here?" Kate whispered.

Bacchus sniffed at around the room and uttered a low growl.

"Even Bacchus is unnerved by this." Kate wrapped an arm around her middle, her gun still pointed at the room, though it was empty of the person who'd done the damage.

Kate pulled her cellphone out of her back pocket and called dispatch. "Hi, Ava. Kate Bradley here. I need to report a break-in." She paused. "At my apartment. Lola Engel's garage apartment on Main Street."

Once Kate finished her report, she ended the call and stared around at the mess. When she started to reach for a chair that was lying on its side, Chance caught her hand. "Don't."

"It's not going to get cleaned up on its own."

"Get what you need for tonight. You're coming with me."

She frowned. "Where? I don't have another place to go. This was it."

"You have two choices. Tonight, you can either stay out at the ranch or at the station, until we can figure out your next move."

"Where will you be?" Kate asked, her voice soft and almost a little lost.

"I can be at the ranch. All I have to do is call Big Mike." Chance reached for his cellphone.

"Won't the guys mind if I'm at the station?"

"We have separate rooms to sleep in at the station," Chance said. "You can have mine. I'll drag a cot out into the kitchen."

She shook her head. "Does your room have an extra cot?"

"Any room can have an extra cot," he said. "We have a stash of army cots in the storeroom, in case we have to have all the volunteers on call for an extended period of time. Or in case we have to turn the station into an emergency shelter for the community."

"Then I'd like to sleep in your room on the extra cot." She stared at the mess around her. For a second, her bottom lip trembled. Then she drew in a deep breath and squared her shoulders. "Just for the night. I'll figure out what to do in the morning."

Chance admired her ability to roll with the

punches, but he could tell she was tired, and the shock was setting in. He gathered her into his arms and held her for a long moment without saying a word.

She wrapped her arms around his waist and leaned her forehead against his chest. They remained still, not saying a word, just holding each other.

Finally, Chance tipped her chin up and stared into her eyes. "It's going to be okay."

Giving him a shaky smile, she nodded. "I know."

Footsteps pounded up the stairs, and Nash appeared at the door. "Kate? Are you all right?"

Kate stepped out of Chance's arms and turned a brave smile toward her trainer. "I'm fine. But I can't say the same for Lola's apartment."

"Son of a bitch." Nash glanced around the room, shaking his head. "Ava notified me as soon as she got the call. Sheriff Olson is on his way. Any idea who might have done this?"

She shook her head. "Not a clue. I haven't even made my first arrest in Hellfire."

"What about the ex-boyfriend?" Chance asked.

Kate shrugged. "I don't even know if he's out of jail yet."

"We can find out soon enough." Nash pressed the button on his radio and asked Ava to put a call out to the police department in San Antonio to get status. "What's his name?"

"Randy Stewart," Kate offered.

After Nash ended the call to Ava, he looked around the small apartment. "We'll process the crime scene, if you want to get out of here and get some rest. You've had a pretty rough day."

Kate started to shake her head, but Chance hooked her elbow with his hand before she could.

Chance placed a hand at the small of her back. "I'm taking her to the station where she can stay the night."

"Why not take her to the ranch?" Nash asked. "There's plenty of room. Becket and Kinsey would be happy to make up a room for her."

"I want to stay in town for now," Kate said. "Until tomorrow. I'll figure out what to do then."

Nash nodded. "Go. I'll take care of securing the apartment once we've dusted for prints."

"Thanks." Kate gave him a half-smile. "This isn't quite how I pictured the end of my first week on the job."

"It's not your fault someone decided to ransack your apartment," Nash said.

Chance scowled. "He must have done it while we were all working the fire and explosions."

"Do you think the two events were related?" Nash asked.

"Makes me wonder," Kate said. "But why would anyone want to ransack my place? It's not like I've lived here long enough to accumulate anything, and I didn't bring much with me."

"We should talk with Lola," Chance suggested. "Maybe she stored something of value in the apartment."

Nash shook his head, frowning. "Why would she keep anything in the garage apartment when she had a big house all to herself?"

"Lola can be eccentric," Chance said. "We'll have to ask her."

Nash shoved a hand through his hair, making it stand on end. "If someone wanted in the apartment, why create a distraction? It was empty for a couple weeks after the fire, and Lola's been staying a couple blocks away in the back of her store."

"Doesn't make sense that someone would go through it now," Nash said. "You don't own any expensive jewelry or art collections, do you?" Chance asked Kate.

"None of that," Kate said. "I barely own much more than the clothes on my back and a couple extra outfits. I left everything in San Antonio for a charity to pick up."

"Then we have to ask Lola." Nash held the door open. "I'll stop by there after the sheriff and I have had a chance to examine what happened here."

"Thanks," Kate said.

Chance took her hand in his and led her through the door and out onto the landing. "We'll be at the fire station if you need to find Kate."

"I'll be at work in the morning, like usual." She

gave Nash a crooked grin. "In jeans and a T-shirt, since my uniform was destroyed in the explosion."

"Do you need to see a doctor?" Nash asked.

"No, I know a medic who can bandage me up, if I need help." She tipped her head toward Chance. "Good night, Nash. See you in the morning."

KATE LET GO of Chance's hand. He descended the stairs in front of her and turned to take her hand again as she came down off the last step.

She didn't argue. The shock of being hit by shrapnel, and then finding her home destroyed, had left her reeling.

"Are you going to be okay?" Chance asked as he opened the passenger door to the truck.

Kate's jaw hardened. She prided herself in being able to handle tough situations. The day had taken its toll, but she wasn't giving up. "I just need a good night's sleep, and I'll be back to normal."

Chance stood by while she climbed up into the truck, favoring her injured leg. Once Kate was inside, he held the back door for Bacchus to climb in. He closed both doors and rounded the pickup to climb into the driver's seat.

Two minutes later, they were back at the station.

Many of the volunteers were still there, finishing cleaning up the equipment and stocking the medical kits. Big Mike, Jace, Bones, Beckett and Rider gathered around Chance, Kate and Bacchus.

"We heard about the home invasion," Beckett said. "We would have come, but Nash radioed back that there was no danger and the space was too small for the whole clan."

"We're glad you'll be staying with us for the night. At least you'll be safe, surrounded by the crew," Rider reached out and hugged Kate. "We're sorry this happened to you."

"It's crappy way to welcome someone to town, if you ask me," Big Mike said and hugged Kate, too. "We already think of you as one of us. And we don't take kindly to people messing with one of our own."

Kate's heart swelled in her chest. "Thanks, guys. This is the first place where I've actually felt at home. And it's all because of you and the folks at the sheriff's department. I just hate that I'm causing trouble for this quiet little town."

Becket snorted and pulled Kate into a bear hug. "Don't believe for a moment that Hellfire is a quiet little town. We've had our share of troubles lately. I believe it's time for our luck to change for the better."

"Agreed," Chance, Rider, Nash and Big Mike all said as one.

"Come on, I'll show you the room I sleep in, and we'll get a cot set up in there." He shot a warning glare at the men standing around. "She's sleeping in my room but not in my bed. I'll be there for moral support. So, can the raunchy comments."

Rider, Jace and Big Mike all held up their hands.

"We don't know what you mean about raunchy comments," Jace Kelly said. "We're all perfect little angels, aren't we?" He backhanded Big Mike in the belly.

The big guy grunted. "Angels," he said and coughed at the same time as he muttered, "In a pig's eye."

Kate loved the way the men all teased and poked at each other and, when the shit hit the fan, how they had their teammates' backs. "I just need a place to sleep for the night. I'll find a place to live tomorrow."

The men straightened up, wiping the smiles from their faces.

"I'll bring a cot from the storeroom up to the room." Big Mike turned and hurried toward a door in the far wall of the bay.

"I'll get extra linens and a pillow," Jace said and hurried in another direction.

Daniel joined them, holding his cellphone to his ear. "Lola said she could be here in two shakes. She's on her way over to the apartment now."

Kate frowned. "Perhaps I need to be there for her."

Daniel listened for a moment, and then met Kate's gaze. "She said not to worry, and that she's sorry this happened to you."

"It wasn't her fault. Somehow, I get the feeling it's mine." Kate felt like she'd stirred up some hornet's nest and set off a chain reaction of some sort, bringing harm to Hellfire. "Someone else did the damage, not her." *Not me.*

"Do you need anything to eat or drink?" Daniel asked. "I have some of that lasagna left in the fridge, or I can cook up an omelet."

"No, thank you. You all have better things to do than wait on me. I'll try not to get in anyone's way, and I'll only stay the one night." Kate looked to Chance. "What I really need is a shower to get all this grime off me."

"I'll show her where the showers are and the fresh towels," Chance said. He cupped her elbow and steered her toward the doors leading into the living quarters and offices.

Kate's feet dragged with every step, and her leg and arm ached. All she wanted was a shower and a bed to lie in. Everything would look better in the morning.

Chance stopped in front of a closet and pulled out a towel and wash cloth. Then he guided her to one of the shower rooms and pushed open the door. "Sorry, we don't have fancy shampoos and conditioners, but there's body wash and shampoo dispensers in the shower stalls."

"I brought my own conditioner. I'll manage."

When he handed her the towel, their hands

touched, and that same jolt of electricity rippled through her tired body. She wanted to fall into his arms and let him hold her until all the bad stuff went away.

She pushed back her shoulders. She couldn't show weakness. Hell, she'd been trained in the military and now was a deputy who could take down a perpetrator, shoot a bad guy and chase criminals without falling apart. Kate slung the towel over her shoulder. "Thanks." She stopped herself from saying so much more. She wasn't ready to tell him how she really felt about him, and he wasn't ready for anyone else in his life. Not when he still mourned Sandy, the love of his life.

Kate entered the bathroom. Bacchus followed and lay on the cool tile floor.

In the shower, Kate quickly scrubbed the parts of her body that hadn't been injured, eased off the bandages that covered the parts that had and rinsed the wounds carefully. After washing her hair, applying conditioner and rinsing thoroughly, she almost felt normal. She did all this quickly. Having limited access to showers in Afghanistan, she'd learned to be quick and efficient when a shower was available. Old habits died hard. And in this case, came in handy.

Less than eight minutes later, she emerged from the shower, wearing one of the T-shirts and a pair of running shorts she'd salvaged from the mess in her apartment. She'd brushed her wet hair back from her forehead and brushed her teeth.

When she and Bacchus left the bathroom, the hallway was empty, but not for long.

"That was quick." Chance emerged from one of the doors farther down the hall. "This is the room I use. You can have the bed. I'll take the cot. The mattress isn't great, but it's marginally better than the cot."

Kate shook her head. "I won't take your bed. I can sleep on the cot."

His jaw tightened, and he held out his hand.

Kate placed hers in his, enjoying the warmth and strength.

"I insist," he said. "You'll be half-asleep by the time I get out of the shower. I don't want to have to crawl across you and Bacchus to get to the bed. I'll sleep on the cot." He stepped back and showed her just how small the room was.

It was only big enough for a twin bed and a cot pushed up against it. They could barely close the door.

Kate smiled. "Is it considered a fire hazard to be that crowded?"

"I'm betting it is, but I won't tell if you don't." He winked and waved her toward the bed. "It has fresh sheets. Get comfortable. I'm going for that shower."

Kate sat on the edge of the cot and scooted backward until she was on the bed, careful not to jostle her leg and start the bleeding all over again. She'd forgotten to ask Chance for additional medical supplies to cover the wounds on her arm and leg. She would ask when he returned from the shower.

Bacchus leaped up onto the cot and crossed to the bed where he curled up at the foot and closed his eyes. Oh, to be a dog and not overthink everything.

In the meantime, Kate lay on top of the blanket, her wet head resting on the pillow. The walls were bare and white. Kate had left the ceiling light on for when Chance finished in the shower and he made his way onto the cot.

She closed her eyes. Flashback images of the fire and explosion immediately crowded her mind, making her wince at the sounds repeating in her head. Kate opened her eyes and stared at the door, willing Chance to hurry in the shower and join her in the little room.

Five minutes later, she heard a door open and close in the hallway. But Chance didn't appear right away. Another door sounded further down the hall.

What was keeping him? Kate sat up and started to scoot toward the end of the bed.

"I'm back." Chance stepped through the door wearing running shorts and a black T-shirt with Hellfire Fire Department written in bright gold letters across the front. "And I came bearing gifts." He grinned and set a variety of medical supplies on the end of the cot. Then he climbed across the little cot to sit on the edge of the bed with Kate. Bacchus sniffed his bare knee and laid his head down, unconcerned about the intruder near his person.

"I can take care of myself," Kate insisted.

"And deprive me of showing off my EMT skills?" He shook his head, dabbed some antibiotic cream onto the torn skin and opened a packet of gauze pads. Folding a couple over, he laid them over the wound on her leg. He tore off a piece of white tape and secured the gauze in place. Then he moved to the arm and used butterfly bandages to pull the edges of the wound together into a tight seam.

When he was done, he looked up. "Better?"

Short of him kissing her boo-boo... "Yes." She stared into his face, her heart thundering in her chest. Every fiber of her being wished he would lean forward and kiss her like he'd probably kissed Sandy a hundred times. Kate just wanted one more kiss.

Oh, who was she lying to? She wanted more than one more kiss. She wanted a lifetime of kisses. She drew her knee up to her chin and slipped her legs beneath the sheets. "You'd better get some sleep."

"You, too." He gathered the medical supplies and disappeared from the room.

While he was gone, Kate settled against the pillow and waited for him to return. Her heart hurt more than her injuries ever could. She was falling for a man who still loved a ghost.

When she heard him speak to someone in the hall,

she closed her eyes and pretended to have drifted off to sleep.

The scent of his cologne wafted to her in the tight confines of the little room. The door clicked shut, and the light around the seam of her eyelids extinguished. Chance crawled into the cot beside her bed and stretched out.

Kate could almost feel his warmth beside her. How she wanted to touch him, to hold him in her arms. To feel his skin against hers.

Then he reached out, patting the edge of her bed until he found her hand. He wrapped his fingers around hers and held them gently.

Kate lay quietly in the darkness. The occasional sound of other voices drifted through the door, but she felt as if she and Chance were alone in their own tiny world where only they existed for the few short hours until daylight.

She held onto that hand, pretending the gesture meant more than just a friend comforting another friend. In her fantasy, his touch was that of a lover, caring for the most important person in his life after a tragic event.

A smile curled her lips as Kate faded into the abyss of sleep where all her dreams came true and no dead woman could reclaim the heart of the man she loved.

CHAPTER 11

FOR A LONG TIME THAT NIGHT, Chance lay awake, sorting through all that had happened that day, that week…hell, since Kate came to town. The day she'd arrived, he'd been thrown off balance, even more than when Bacchus had knocked him on his ass. That had been the beginning of what felt like a transition.

The question he asked himself was what had he transitioned from and to?

All the words his siblings had thrown at him that night Kate had come to dinner at the ranch came back to him. His family had encouraged him to date. To get out there again. To find someone to love. They'd seen him as the empty shell of the man he'd become and didn't want him to continue to live half a life.

For the two years following Sandy's death, he had been living in a vacuum. Getting out of the military and returning to his home in Hellfire hadn't been enough to set him free from his demons. In the one week Kate had been in town, he'd come further than the entire two years he'd been home. She'd woken him to the possibilities of finding someone he could love as much, if not more than Sandy. At the very least, someone he could love differently. Sandy would always be in his heart. She'd been his first love, and he would never forget her. But he'd lived when she'd died.

Sandy wouldn't have wanted him to mourn her forever. She would have been the first to tell him to shake out of it and get the hell on with living. He lay in the cot, thinking about Sandy—only the good memories. Not the last few minutes of her life, when he'd held her as she'd died in his arms. He remembered the smiling, happy Sandy who'd loved with all of her heart and hated to see anyone in physical or emotional pain.

As he held Kate's hand, he could almost imagine Sandy smiling down at him…at last. She would have been happy for him to have found someone he cared about.

Kate had insisted they remain friends. If that was what she wanted, he would be that friend to her. For a while. In the meantime, he would show her how loyal and caring he could be, unlike the loser of a boyfriend, who'd betrayed her trust and taken advantage of her while she'd been deployed.

His free hand clenched into a fist. If he ever met the bastard…

Kate's hand tightened in his. Her fingers were strong, yet supple, like her. She could run like the wind but got excited about a miniature horse.

If she could love him half as much as she loved her dog, he would consider himself a lucky man.

He slipped into a troubled sleep, where his dreams consisted of exploding buildings where Kate was injured, perhaps dying. His heart squeezed tightly in his chest, and he fought to breathe in air thick with smoke and destruction. She couldn't die. He couldn't bear to lose her. Though he'd only known her for a week, deep down he knew she was someone he could love for as long as they both should live.

He woke before dawn, Kate's hand still in his. She lay on her good side, facing him, her breathing slow and steady. But she was breathing.

Chance heaved a sigh and lay in the limited light coming from beneath the door, staring at the silhouette of the woman beside him. This living, breathing woman cared about people and had risked her life to save them when she could have been killed herself.

Kate and Sandy were nothing alike in looks. Sandy had been blond-haired and blue-eyed. Kate had richly dark hair and incredible green eyes. As different as they were in looks, they were more alike in spirit. Both were willing to take risks with their lives by joining the military. Kate continued to take risks by signing on with the sheriff's department. They were both brave in their own ways and wanted to be a part of something bigger than they were as individuals. Perhaps that was what had drawn Chance to both. He, too, had wanted to be a part of something bigger than himself. In the military, he'd given back to his country. As a firefighter, he helped protect his community.

Bacchus stirred and sat up.

Not wanting to disturb Kate, Chance reluctantly released her hand and eased himself off the cot as quietly as he could. He opened the door and motioned for Bacchus to follow.

The dog leaped to the floor and trotted alongside Chance as they walked down the hallway to the exit.

Once outside, the dog relieved himself, sniffed at the plants and shrubs for a few minutes, and then returned to Chance's side.

"I bet you're thirsty." Chance led Bacchus back into the kitchen where he found a bowl, filled it with water and set it on the floor.

The dog spent a full minute lapping at the water, splashing droplets over the edge. When he was satisfied, he looked up at Chance and turned toward the hallway where the bedrooms were.

Kate stood there, wearing her tennis shoes, her hair pulled back in a ponytail. "Are we going for our run this morning?" she asked.

"Are you sure you should with that gash in your leg?"

She nodded. "It feels better already. And it wasn't very deep, only a scratch."

Knowing he wouldn't talk her out of it, and not wanting her to run on her own, Chance nodded. "Give me a second to grab my shoes and my radio. I can't go far from the station."

"We can jog around town to keep us closer," she said.

Chance hurried to get his shoes and returned a couple minutes later, ready to go.

They jogged in silence.

With his feelings still very close to the surface and kind of raw, Chance couldn't voice any of them. And he was afraid that if he declared his growing attraction to her, he'd scare Kate away. She'd said on multiple occasions she wasn't interested in starting a relationship after having failed so miserably with her last one.

What she didn't understand was that she hadn't failed. Her ex had been a complete ass and didn't deserve to walk on the same ground as Kate. The man needed someone to kick his ass for what he'd done to Kate.

All those words roiled up inside Chance as he ran alongside Kate and Bacchus.

Her face was set in a grim determination as she kept a steady pace.

By the time they'd returned to the station, Chance could barely stand the silence. "Kate," he said as they walked the last block. "We need to talk."

She frowned down at her shoes. "Maybe. But does it have to be now?" She looked up, but not at him.

The station was within earshot, and some of the guys were outside spraying some of the gear down that had been used in the fire the night before. They would let it dry in the sun, and then pack it away later.

"No. Can we meet for dinner tonight? I'll be off duty after breakfast."

She hesitated, her hand going to Bacchus's head. After she scratched the ruff of his neck, she finally responded, "Okay."

"I'll pick you up from the sheriff's office when you get off work."

She nodded, her lips quirking. "That's just as well, since I don't know where I'll be hanging my hat tonight. I have to work on that today."

They entered the station where breakfast was cooking. Bones had control of the kitchen and was issuing orders to whoever was standing nearby to set the table and pop more bread into the toaster.

Kate slipped through to the room where she'd stashed her things and hit the shower. Bacchus stayed in the kitchen with Chance, possibly hoping for some bites of bacon from a softhearted Bones.

Less than five minutes later, Kate appeared

dressed in jeans, a sheriff's department T-shirt and a pair of black combat boots. Her long dark hair was pulled straight back from her forehead into a tight ponytail at the nape of her neck.

She looked absolutely badass and took Chance's breath away.

"Wow, Bradley," Daniel said. "You look like you could kick some serious ass today."

She smiled, softening the hardcore image and melting Chance's heart in the process. He wasn't sure he could wait until dinner that night to have that talk. Then again, at least he'd have another full day to enjoy before he scared her off.

She grabbed a piece of toast from the stack and headed for the door.

"Aren't you staying for breakfast?" Bones asked before Chance could get the words out.

She held up the toast. "This is it. Thanks for your hospitability. I hope to find another place to live by this evening, so you won't have to put up with me."

"Are you kidding?" Daniel shook his head as he buttered another batch of toast. "You're a lot better looking than Grayson's ugly mug." He winked. "Go get the bad guys. We're here if you need us."

Chance walked her out the door, wishing he felt as if he could joke with her as easily as his friend. Instead, he felt as if he were walking on eggshells, and anything he had to say would make her end things with him on the spot. That evening, he'd tell her how he felt. If she didn't feel the same, she'd tell him. Then he'd at least know where he stood. If there was hope, and she wanted to explore the possibilities at a slower pace, he could do that, too. He wasn't ready to give up on something that, in his mind, was just beginning.

Kate left the station with her backpack slung over her shoulder, Bacchus on a lead beside her.

Chance watched until they disappeared a couple blocks away into the sheriff's office.

When he went back inside the station, Daniel met him with a mug of coffee. "Here, you look like you could use some caffeine."

"You know me well," he said and took the steaming mug from his friend.

"Sit down, have some breakfast and tell me what's going through that mind of yours. You look like you're about to lose your best friend."

He sighed. "That's what I'm afraid of."

CHAPTER 12

KATE SPENT the first part of the day riding with Nash in the service SUV, checking on the burn site, her apartment and other areas of town. They answered a couple calls, one about a horse loose on a country road. They'd herded the animal back into its fence and talked with the owner about shoring up the gate it had escaped through. Another call was from a woman who was certain someone had stolen the diamond necklace her husband had given to her on their fiftieth wedding anniversary.

Kate and Nash had helped her search her house for the missing necklace only to find it where she'd left it—hidden in a secret drawer where she'd been sure no one would think to look for it. Apparently, she hadn't remembered putting it there, until she'd found it.

After noon, Nash had paperwork to do in the

office, which gave Kate time to work with Bacchus behind the building. She'd checked out a canvas bag with trace amounts of cocaine inside.

Bacchus had responded well to detecting cannabis no matter where she'd hidden it. He was even getting used to sitting instead of lying down when he detected drugs. She'd switched several times between the drugs and the C4 to make certain he detected the difference.

As always, Bacchus was smart—and Kate couldn't fully accept credit for how quickly he learned.

An hour into training with the cocaine, Bacchus was finding it hidden in the different places she could leave it...beneath a stack of pallets, under the stack of tires and beneath her backpack she'd brought along to use as a different place to hide the drugs.

Each time, Bacchus sniffed around the perimeter and eventually found the drug.

"Kate?" Nash poked his head out the back door. "Sheriff Olson and I are headed over to the burn site to meet folks from the state crime lab. You can come or stay. We won't be long."

"I'd like to finish up with Bacchus, unless you think it would be better for me to go with you." She'd just hidden the cocaine for the fourth time near the base of the office building, behind an old flower pot near a water spigot. She'd led Bacchus to the far end

of the building to start the search when Nash had
announced his intention.

"Then stay. We won't be gone long. If we aren't
back by quitting time, I'll see you Monday."

Kate nodded. "Have a good weekend." She hadn't
wanted to tell him that she needed to be at the sheriff's office at quitting time because she had a date
with Nash's brother. If she'd gone with Nash and the
sheriff, she might have missed Chance coming by to
pick her up.

Determined to wrap up her training session and
have enough time to wash her hands and comb her
hair, Kate urged Bacchus to continue his search for
the cocaine pouch.

This time, she took him away from the building
and had him sniff the old vehicles parked in the back
lot and the storage building where they kept some
equipment and where she'd left her grandmother's
desk. She was glad the desk hadn't been in the apartment when it had been ransacked. It wouldn't have
fared well in the amount of destruction that had
taken place.

She'd talked with Lola about finding another
place to stay. Lola had offered her a rollaway cot in
the back of her shop until she could get someone in
to clean up the mess and replace the furnishings that
had been damaged.

Lola had been so kind and apologetic, Kate had
felt bad for the woman. She'd lost her home to a fire,

and now someone had destroyed the apartment she'd rented out. How unlucky could one woman be?

"The worst part," Lola had confided, "was losing my entire shoe collection in the fire." She sighed sadly. Then she'd perked up. "But that gave me an excuse to buy all new ones."

Kate had laughed. She didn't understand Lola's love of beautiful shoes, but she liked Lola. "I can sleep on a rollaway cot. I've slept on worse."

"Then I'll see you after you get off work?" Lola had said.

"Later. I'm going to catch a bite to eat before I come by the shoe store." She didn't say she had a date. She wasn't really sure what her meeting with Chance was. He'd only said they needed to talk, and he would take her to dinner to do it.

Her gut clenched. What if he was going to break it to her that he couldn't keep seeing her as a friend? Hell, she didn't want to keep seeing him as a friend. Her feelings for him had grown exponentially in the past week. It scared her how much she liked him. At this point, she was even more afraid of losing him. If she shared her feelings, would he turn and run away as fast as he could? Hell, he wasn't over the death of his first love.

Kate had all those thoughts going through her head when Bacchus dropped to a sitting position in front of the storage shed and looked up at her.

She frowned at the shed and looked down at

Bacchus's expectant face. "There's not any cocaine in the shed." She tugged on his lead, but he refused to get up, sitting stoically in front of the shed, his tongue lolling, waiting for her to give him his toy.

Kate had a spare key to the shed on her key ring in her pocket. "Okay, we'll look, but I'm telling you, the cocaine isn't in the shed." She had nearly thirty minutes to spare before Chance was due to pick her up. It wouldn't hurt to take Bacchus through the shed to prove he'd been mistaken. Perhaps the cocaine training would take longer than the marijuana.

Kate unlocked the shed door and opened it wide.

A jumble of equipment was stored inside, from gardening tools used to maintain the grounds of the office, to old desks, crow bars and shovels. To one side stood a couple of boxes of her photo albums and memorabilia and her grandmother's secretary desk.

Bacchus let out a low, dangerous growl.

"What's wrong, boy?" Kate's gaze shifted from the desk to the dog sitting at her feet.

Instead of facing into the shed, Bacchus had turned around, the hairs on the back of his neck stood at attention, and his mouth curled into a wicked snarl.

"Kate, you might want to control your dog," an all too familiar voice said.

She spun to face Randy, her heart sinking to her knees when she realized he held a gun in his hand.

"If that dog takes one step toward me, I'll shoot him," Randy warned. "Then I'll shoot you."

Bacchus growled again, low in his throat.

"Bacchus, *platz*," Kate ordered, her hand tightening on his lead. "What do you want, Randy?"

"I want what's mine," he said.

"I don't have anything that belongs to you. Hell, I don't have anything of value. Don't you think you're being a little ridiculous with that gun?" She shook her head. "Do you even know how to use it?"

"I know how to use the gun. I point, pull the trigger and a bullet comes out." He aimed at Bacchus. "Do anything stupid, and I'll kill your precious dog."

Bacchus released a threatening rumble from deep in his chest.

"You don't know what kind of trouble you started," Randy said, his lips twisting in a snarl.

"Apparently, I don't. Why don't you tell me about it," she said, playing for time while she searched for a way out of the bind she was in. Sheriff Olson and Nash Grayson had gone to the site of the previous day's fire and explosion. They wouldn't be back for at least another thirty minutes.

Ava, the dispatcher, was glued to her monitors and the 911 phone system. She wouldn't be able to break free to check on Kate, nor would she suspect anything was wrong if Kate didn't come back into the office. Her job was to focus on any 911 calls coming in from all over the county.

Which left Kate alone with Bacchus, and her ex-boyfriend threatening to kill the dog.

Kate would be damned if she let Randy harm one hair on Bacchus's head. "Tell me what you want. Maybe I can help you find it."

"I know where it is, now. I just need to get it to the right people before they decide I've absconded with it to get a better deal."

Kate shook her head, an even deeper feeling of dread washing over her. "What are you talking about?"

"The package I hid in that hunk-of-junk desk that belonged to your grandmother." He waved the gun at the interior of the shed. "Now that I've found it, all I have to do is get the package to the buyer, and I'm off the hook."

Kat's mouth pressed into a thin line. "You were dealing drugs out of my apartment?"

"I couldn't get a decent job. How do you think I could afford to live?"

"You were living rent-free on me."

"Yeah, rent-free, but not free. I still had to eat and pay for my car and gas."

"Wow, Randy, you are a piece of work."

"Yeah, and you're all holier than everyone." He took a step closer, his gun pointing at Bacchus. "Shut up and get into the shed, and take your dog in there, too."

"What are you going to do?" she asked as she backed into the shed, dragging Bacchus with her.

"It's not what I'm going to do, but what you're going to do." He nodded toward the desk. "You remember the secret drawer you showed me in your grandmother's desk?"

She nodded.

"Open it."

She hesitated. "Why? What's in it?"

"Open it, damn it, or the dog dies," he said, his tone intense, sweat popping out on his brow.

Kate did as she was instructed. She figured as long as he wasn't shooting, she was okay. She needed to drag out the encounter as long as she could until help had a chance to arrive.

Chance. As her thoughts went to the firefighter, she realized he could show up there unarmed and try to rescue her.

Randy was unhinged enough he would shoot anyone who surprised him from behind.

Kate dropped down the front of the desk, creating a desktop for writing letters. Then she reached into one of the cubbies and pressed a dowel button. The button released a drawer that blended into the design of the desk. When it popped out, a bag filled with white powder came with it.

Kate gasped. "That was in there this whole time?"

"Why do you think I was so adamant about

getting my things before you had the police cart me off?"

"You bastard. The whole time I was in a war zone, you were using me and my apartment to deal drugs, knowing how I feel about them."

"You're just a stupid goody-two-shoes. You don't know what it's like to be jobless. You don't get it."

"Yeah," Kate snorted. "Because I could always find work. I'm not too proud to flip burgers or clean toilets."

"Well, I'm not going to clean up after other people's shit." He waved with his free hand. "Bring me the stuff."

Kate wanted to throw it in his face, but he still had his gun pointed at Bacchus. She couldn't risk it. Randy might get trigger-happy and shoot the dog.

She walked toward the man she'd wasted too many days of her life with. When she came close enough to hand him the cocaine, he grabbed her outstretched hand, spun her around and yanked her against him, wrapping his arm around her neck in a headlock.

Bacchus braced to lunge.

"Bacchus, *platz!*" Kate yelled, afraid the dog would try to protect her and catch a bullet for his efforts.

"That's right. Tell that dog to stay," Randy said, his breath hot in Kate's ear. "If you want him to live, you'll close the shed with him in it."

Kate saw it as the only way to keep the dog safe.

Once she was certain Bacchus wouldn't be harmed, she'd figure a way out of Randy's grip.

Randy inched forward with her as she swung the shed door closed with her free hand. She still held the cocaine in her other hand.

When the door was closed and secured with Bacchus safely inside, she swung the cocaine up and behind her, hoping it was in the direction of Randy's face.

He ducked, and the brick of drugs sailed past him and landed with a thud on the ground.

Randy tightened his arm around Kate's neck. "I still have a gun, only now it's pointed at your head. After spending the last few days in jail, I can tell you it wouldn't take much for me to put a bullet through your head."

"Take your drugs and go," she said, her voice barely above a whisper. She couldn't get enough air into her lungs, much less past her vocal cords.

"Oh, I'm taking the drugs, all right." He lifted her off her feet, tilting back with his arm still around her neck.

Kate clutched at his arm, trying to drag it down so that she could breathe. He set her on her feet in front of the cocaine and loosened his hold. "Get the stuff," he commanded. "And don't try throwing it again. I can still pump a lot of bullets into the door of that shed. The dog didn't have much room to move in there." He leaned close, his mouth near her ear. "Get the picture?"

"Bastard," she said. "Leave the dog alone." Bending with him, she retrieved the cocaine from the ground. "You have what you came for. If you don't leave soon, others will come looking for me."

"Then get moving. We don't have much time." He waved the gun toward the alley beside the sheriff's office. Still holding her tightly, he maneuvered her around the corner. A dark sedan stood in the shadows of the alley.

"Get in," Randy said. "You're driving."

She dug her feet into the pavement, bringing them to a halt out of range of the shed and Bacchus. Already the dog was barking and scratching at the door. Kate could hear his desperation, even as muffled as the sound was. She had to get away and free her dog. The shed could get hot enough to be dangerous in the late-afternoon Texas sun.

"Move or die, bitch," Randy ordered, pressing the gun to her temple.

Kate knew if she got in that vehicle, she would have less than a fifty-percent chance of living. At that exact moment, no one knew Randy was in town. No one would see him driving off with Kate in his car. The car wasn't anything Kate recognized and was probably stolen.

If she didn't do something now, she might not live to rescue Bacchus from the heat of the sealed shed.

Remembering as much of her hand-to-hand combat training as she could, she slammed her arm up against the barrel of the pistol. The gun went off, but the bullet missed her. Jabbing her elbow into Randy's midsection, she tucked her chin into her chest and ducked beneath his arm as he loosened his grip.

Kate dove, grabbed hold of his wrist and pushed the gun up in the air.

Randy fired again. "Damn you to hell. I should have blown up your apartment with you and that damned dog of yours in it."

"You! You were responsible for the explosions?" she gritted out, still wrestling to keep the gun raised.

"Damn right I was. I gave some teenagers drugs for their explosives. Made for some impressive fire-works. No one saw me go into your apartment. They were too busy worrying about the fire and the explosions."

Fury fueled Kate's efforts. She released her hold on his wrist and slammed her palm into his nose.

Randy cursed and swung his arm, his aim off as he blinked tears from his eyes. Blood ran from his broken nose and down his chin. He roared his anger and aimed toward Kate.

She dove for the ground, but not soon enough. A bullet caught her as she fell. Pain knifed through her side. She couldn't let it stop her. She couldn't die.

Bacchus needed her. And she had a date with a man she was falling hopelessly in love with.

Another shot was fired, hitting her in the shoulder. Pain racked her body as she dragged herself away from the man, heading for the corner and some measure of cover from flying bullets.

As she rounded the corner, she looked back.

Randy wiped blood from his face with the back of his hand and reached for the brick of cocaine that had rolled to a stop near the sedan.

As he picked up the packet, the wrapping disintegrated in his hands and white powder exploded in all directions.

"No!" Randy cried. He dropped to his knees and raked at the dust, trying to pull it back together. Wind picked up and blew the dust up and into a swirl, and then whipped it away. Randy roared and turned toward Kate. "You bitch! You stupid bitch! Do you know what you've done?" The hate and loathing in Randy's eyes were so vivid, Kate shivered.

The man staggered to his feet, lifted the gun, aiming again at Kate.

With little energy left, Kate couldn't crawl the rest of the way around the corner. So, she tucked her arms close to her sides and rolled.

Shots rang out. Kate couldn't feel any new pain, but darkness closed in on her, fading her vision to black, her last thoughts of Bacchus and Chance.

CHAPTER 13

CHANCE COUNTED every minute throughout the day, anxious to see Kate and to tell her how he felt. He prayed she wouldn't spook and tell him she didn't want to see him ever again. Hoped she would at least let him woo her, taking his time to win her over. He'd be patient, if he knew he had even a slim chance of Kate eventually falling in love with him.

Just the thought of giving his heart to Kate made the world look entirely different to him. Gone was the darkness he'd carried with him since Sandy's death. It was as if the sun had finally come out in Hellfire, and it was shining down on him with hope and promise of better days to come.

Thirty minutes before he was supposed to be at the sheriff's office, he couldn't wait another minute. He drove his motorcycle to the front of the office, disappointed that not a single SUV stood out front. Would Kate be out on a call and late getting back? God, he hoped not. Everything he wanted to say was fighting to get out of him. If he held it in much longer, he'd explode.

He parked his motorcycle, got off and slipped out of his helmet. He laid it next to the one he'd brought for Kate. She'd said she wanted a ride on his bike. Though he'd wanted to take her horseback riding first, he didn't want to disappoint her when so much was at stake.

Like a teen on his first date, he shuffled his feet and worried she might not be as taken with him as he was with her.

Then he heard a sound he hadn't heard since he'd returned from the war in Afghanistan.

Gunfire.

His blood ran cold, and he turned in the direction he thought it had come from. He stared at the sheriff's office. The sound had come from somewhere around the building. It hadn't been muffled, so it couldn't have come from inside.

He started running, even as his mind played through different scenarios. Who could be firing a gun so close to the office?

Another shot echoed off the walls of the nearby buildings.

Chance entered the alley between the sheriff's

office and the building next to it. A dark gray sedan was parked in the shadows. A man pushed to his feet with his back to Chance, cursing as white dust flew around his head. He lifted his arms.

Chance could see he had a gun in his hands. He didn't recognize the guy and, in a split-second, concluded he was a threat.

Chance ran toward the man and hit him in the back like a linebacker taking out the opposing quarterback. The gun in the guy's hand went off.

Chance landed on the man's back, slamming his face into the pavement. The pistol slid across the ground, coming to a stop a couple of yards away.

The shooter lay still, unmoving. Breathing, but unconscious.

Chance pushed to his feet and stared down at the man, and then in the direction he'd been pointing.

A swath of blood streaked the pavement in bright red.

His heart pounded as he swept the gun up in his hand and followed the trail of blood.

As Chance rounded the corner his heart plummeted to his gut, and he dropped to his knees.

Kate lay on her side on the ground, blood staining the T-shirt she'd left the fire station in that morning.

Chance touched his fingers to the base of her throat and let out the breath he'd been holding when he felt a pulse. "Kate, sweetheart. Can you hear me?"

he asked, his voice shaking. Hell, his hands shook, and his eyes burned. God, she couldn't die on him. From the blood oozing out of her, she'd been hit in the shoulder and in the side.

Chance stripped out of the jacket he'd worn and pulled off his T-shirt. He ripped it into pieces and formed a couple of pads he pressed into the wounds. "Oh, baby, I should have come earlier. I should have been here for you."

Her eyes blinked open, and she stared up at him. "Chance?"

"I'm here, sweetheart."

Her gaze darted left then right. "It was Randy. He has a gun." She tried to sit up, but Chance held her steady.

"He doesn't have it anymore. I took it from him."

She slumped in his arms, and her eyes closed, only to open again. "Bacchus. You have to get Bacchus."

"Where is he?"

She looked past him. "In the shed."

That's when Chance heard the barking and the scratching. Until then, all he'd been able to focus on was Kate lying on the ground, bleeding out.

"He'll be okay."

She shook her head. "No, please. Let him out. It's hot. He could die."

"Darlin', if I let go of the pressure on your wounds, you could die."

"Rather me than him," she said, her voice fading. Then she struggled to sit up. "Please, let him out."

Chance struggled with what to do. If he refused to let the dog out, she'd get up and let him out herself. Either way, she'd bleed out. Probably faster if she got up and tried to free the dog.

"Promise me you'll lie still until I get back."

She nodded. "Help Bacchus."

He took her hands and positioned them over the wounds the best he could. "Hold those there until I get back."

She nodded. "Hurry."

Chance staggered to his feet and ran toward the shed. When he ripped open the door, the dog leaped out.

A cry sounded behind him. He turned in time to see Randy standing over Kate with a knife in his hand.

Bacchus raced toward Kate's attacker and sank his teeth into the arm holding the knife.

Randy screamed and staggered backward. He tripped and fell to the ground, crying out for help.

Chance didn't have any sympathy for the man. He hoped the dog tore him apart for what he'd done to Kate.

He ran back to Kate to find her passed out, her hands having slid off the wounds, blood seeping once again onto the ground.

"Help!" he called out, afraid to leave Kate for fear

ELLE JAMES

she'd lose too much blood and die. His worst night-
mare seemed to be happening all over again. First,
he'd lost Sandy to a gunshot wound. Now, he could
very well lose Kate. He'd be damned if that
happened.

"Kate, sweetheart, wake up. Tell me you're going
to be okay. We have a date tonight."

Her eyes fluttered but remained closed. "A date?"
she whispered.

He laughed, the sound catching on a sob. "If you
want it to be."

"Do you?" she asked, her voice so soft, he could
barely hear her words over the sound of Bacchus
growling at Randy.

"Help!" the other man called out. "Get this dog
off me."

Kate opened her eyes and stared up into Chance's,
waiting for his reply.

"I want it to be the first of many dates with you,
Kate Bradley. But I don't want to scare you off. If
you're not ready, I can wait. I can be very patient, if
you let me be."

Her lips formed a weak smile. "I'm not afraid."

"I promise, I'm not like your ex," he said, glaring at
the man struggling with the dog, ripping at his arm.
"I'll kill the bastard. Just say the word."

Kate shook her head. "He's not worth you going
to jail." She turned her head. "Bacchus, *platz*." Her
voice didn't carry far enough for the dog to hear.

Drawing in a deep breath, she tried again. "Bacchus, *platz*!

The dog gave one last good shake before he released his hold on the man's arm.

"Bacchus, *sitz*."

The dog sat in front of Randy, growling, his teeth bared.

"Good dog," Kate said and collapsed in Chance's arms.

"We need to get you to the hospital."

At that moment, Nash and Sheriff Olson appeared from around the corner.

As soon as he saw what had happened, Nash was on his radio, calling for an ambulance.

Sheriff Olson and Nash cuffed Randy and led him around to the front of the building.

A siren wailed as the ambulance arrived from the fire station. Nash led the EMTs to the back of the building. Daniel and Big Mike followed with the stretcher.

While the medical technicians took over Kate's care, Chance moved back, watching over her as they worked to stop the bleeding and hook her up to an IV.

Once they had her stabilized, they loaded her onto the stretcher and hurried her toward the waiting ambulance.

Chance gathered Bacchus's lead and followed alongside the stretcher, holding Kate's hand.

"Bacchus?"

"Is with me."

"They won't let him come to the hospital?"

"He's coming." Chance knew the guys. If he said the dog had to come, they'd let the dog come.

"You'll be there, too?" she asked.

"Wild horses couldn't keep me away," he said.

She chuckled, the sound catching in her throat. "Hell of a first date, huh?"

"Can't say it wasn't exciting."

"I could use a little less excitement." Kate closed her eyes, a smile curling the corners of her lips. "Randy set off the explosions. Like you said, as a distraction. He was looking for cocaine he hid in my grandmother's desk."

"I'll relay that to the sheriff."

The rest of the trip to the hospital was accomplished in silence as the EMTs worked to keep Kate stabilized.

She faded in and out of consciousness. Each time, Chance worried that she wouldn't wake up. He held her hand in his, praying for a miracle.

Once they reached the hospital, Kate was whisked off to an operating room. Chance and Bacchus were shown to the waiting room. Nash, Rider, Becket, Sheriff Olson, Kinsey, Lola, Phoebe and Chance's mother and father arrived shortly after and gathered around Chance. No one talked. Each one of them hugged Chance and took a seat to wait with him.

By the time the surgeon finally emerged, Chance was beside himself with worry.

The doctor looked around the waiting room. "Family of Miss Bradley?"

"That's us." Chance stood with Bacchus.

"She's going to be all right. The bullets missed all her vital organs. She'll have to have some physical therapy for the shoulder. With a little work, she should have a full recovery."

Chance nearly wept with relief. His family gathered around him, smiling, sharing his relief.

"She's going to be okay," his mother said, and hugged him tight. "I'm so glad. I like her a lot. She'll be a good addition to our family."

"Can she have visitors?" Chance asked the surgeon.

The surgeon looked around at the full waiting room. "Hospital rule is only two at a time."

"Come Bacchus," Chance said.

The doctor frowned. "Dogs aren't allowed."

"He's not a dog." Chance said. "He's family."

The doctor smiled. "Whatever aids recovery."

Chance and Bacchus spent the rest of the night sitting at Kate's bedside.

Chance wanted to be there when she woke. He wanted her to know Bacchus was taken care of and that she didn't have to worry about Randy ever again. He still wanted to have that conversation with her, but it could wait until she was feeling better.

She'd wanted their dinner to be a first date.

His heart swelled with hope and love for the woman lying in the bed beside him. She wasn't completely out of the woods yet, but when she was, he was going to kiss her like there'd be no tomorrow.

CHAPTER 14

THREE WEEKS LATER.

KATE LAY on the clean white sheets on the new mattress she and Chance had purchased when they'd moved together into Lola's renovated garage apartment. They'd decided to live there for the time being as they got to know each other better.

Chance had promised to take it slow with Kate, letting her get used to the idea that he really wanted to be with her. And also to give her wounds time to recover before they took their relationship to a physical level.

Kate had grown frustrated with how slow he was moving and had insisted they move in together. They'd almost had their first fight as a couple over her insistence. He didn't think she was ready. She'd kissed him until he'd agreed to move in.

Chance stirred beside her. "Hey, beautiful." He rested his hand on her hip. "Feeling okay?"

She nodded, and then shook her head. "I'm more than okay and past ready."

"For?" He nuzzled her neck and pressed a kiss to the base of her throat where her pulse beat swiftly, sending heat throughout her body.

"If I have to tell you..." She huffed out a sigh and shoved at his chest. "My wounds are closed, I'm well on my way to a full recovery." She cupped his face in her palm and brushed a kiss across his lips. "I'm ready for you to make love with me."

Chance frowned. "I don't want to reinjure you."

"You're not going to. If anything hurts, I'll tell you." She smoothed her thumb across the wrinkles on his forehead. "I know my limits."

"You might know yours, but I'm not sure that, once we start, I can hold back." He leaned up on his elbow. "I've waited this long, I can wait a little longer, sweetheart."

It was Kate's turn to frown. "Well, I can't wait another minute. If you won't make love to me, I'll just have to make love to you." She rolled over on top of him and pulled her nightgown up over her head. Straddling his hips, she stared down at him, her naked breasts there for him to feast on. "Am I getting through to you?"

He reached up, cupped her breasts in his hands and groaned. "Sweetheart, you had my attention from the first day we met."

She laughed. "Bacchus had your attention. I was an afterthought."

"He did knock me on my ass, but you were the reason I hung around." He gripped her bottom in his hands and lifted her off him.

Kate pouted. "I can't tempt you in the least?"

"Oh, I'm beyond tempted," he said, "but it would help if we were both completely naked before we start." And to prove his point, he rose from the bed, stripped out of his shorts and stood before her in all of his masculine glory. "I wanted everything to be perfect, so I could show you how good we could be together."

"I have no doubt we'll give this mattress a good workout," she said as she slipped out of her panties and tossed them into a corner. "Come here, big guy. I think we've both stopped running from our pasts. It's time to build a future."

"I couldn't have said it better." He climbed onto the bed and leaned over her, not putting his full weight on her body. "I knew from that first kiss that you were special. It just took me a little longer to realize how very special." He kissed her soundly.

Kate opened to him and swept her tongue across his, deepening their connection. She ran her hands over his back and down to his buttocks. She spread her legs and guided him to lie between them, his shaft pressing against her entrance. "I love you, Chance Grayson," she said. "I didn't think I could fall in love until I met you."

"And I didn't think I could fall in love again, until I found you," Chance said. "I love you, Kate Bradley. You brought me back to a life worth living. Thank you."

"And you showed me there are still real men out there. I was lucky enough to find one. Now, let's set this mattress on fire." She held out her hand. "Condom?"

He slapped one into her palm with a grin.

Kate helped him fit it over his erection, and then gripped his ass and guided him home.

He slid into her and filled up all the empty space she'd had in her body and her heart for far too long. She'd found a home in Hellfire, Texas and a man to love and who loved her. Life didn't get better than that.

She was wrong.

As he moved in and out, she realized, life did get even better. Their lovemaking made the mattress go up in flames. If she'd uttered the thought out loud, it would have sounded corny, but making love with Chance was...life-affirming...glorious. The wonder of it all stole her breath away.

He paused mid-stroke. "You okay, baby?" he whispered, dipping down to kiss her forehead.

"Better than okay." She shook her head. "I've never…"

"I know." He smiled and moved faster. "Baby, hold on."

"Wait," she said. Wrapping her arms around him, she gave him a blinding smile. "I love you."

"You're killing me," he said, his eyes darkening. "I love you, too. Forever."

Together, they moved, heat building between them until it flashed over and consumed them.

COMING SOON

From

New York Times & *USA Today*
Bestselling Author

ELLE JAMES

TOTAL MELTDOWN

HELLFIRE SERIES #7

New York Times & *USA Today*
Bestselling Author

ELLE JAMES

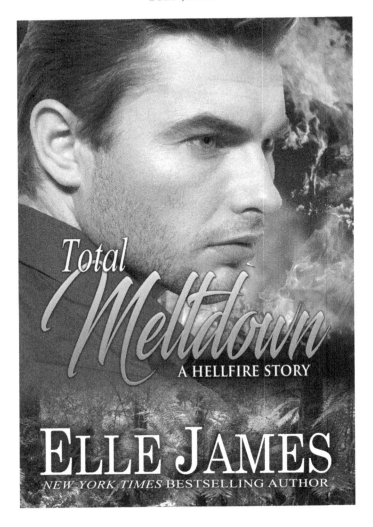

ABOUT TOTAL MELTDOWN......

An elementary teacher during the school year, Lily Grayson hires out as an au pair during the summer in order to travel expenses-paid to exotic locations with wealthy families with children. When one of her students suggests she apply for a summer job with his family going to Costa Rica, she jumps at the chance. Despite her immediate clash with his father, she agrees to accompany him and his two children to the central American country.

Rich Texas rancher originally from Costa Rica, Antonio Delossantos, knows money can't buy everything. He lost his wife to violence and he's determined to save his children from a similar fate. When he learns his son's school teacher is also skilled in Krav Maga military-style self-defense, he agrees to hire her for the summer he intends to spend in Costa Rica.

Lily and Antonio join forces when the children come under attack by terrorists who attempt to kidnap them to hold for ransom. What starts as a summer vacation in a tropical paradise soon becomes a race to survive in the jungles of Costa Rica. Pre-order Total Meltdown Now!

SOLDIER'S DUTY

IRON HORSE LEGACY SERIES #1

New York Times & *USA Today*
Bestselling Author

ELLE JAMES

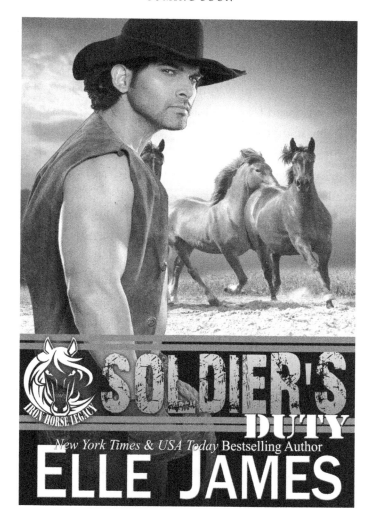

ABOUT SOLDIER'S DUTY......

When their father disappeared into the Crazy Mountains, the McKinnon boys had to grow up fast.

Angus McKinnon, the oldest, had just completed his fourth deployment with the elite Delta Forces when he was called home. He ended his Army career to return to the family ranch and help his mother. He was supposed to come back and marry his girlfriend, but she hadn't waited for him. After he left to join the military, she left, too. Regret burns hot in Angus over leaving his military career and brothers in arms, as well as for losing the girl he loved.

Bree Lansing was brokenhearted when Angus left to join the military. Though she promised to wait for his return on leave, fate played an evil hand. During a confrontation with her stepfather in the barn, he fell and she left vowing never to return. Later she learned the barn burned with her stepfather in it. Bree moves to Alaska and starts a new life there. She refuses to regret her stepfather's death, but fears returning to Montana, afraid she'll be charged with killing him. When her mother falls ill, Bree must return home and face her guilt and fear while keeping the man she once loved at a distance. She can't let him close when her secrets could ruin her life and his, by association.

With Bree back in town, Angus dares to dream of a happily-ever-after. If only he can convince her that he never stopped loving her, even though she didn't wait. What he doesn't understand is how accident-prone she's become since she's returned. When the accidents turn near deadly, he pulls Bree into his protective embrace. Sparks fly and the years melt away, leaving their emotions fiery and raw. Someone is trying to kill Bree, but perhaps more troubling is the desire building between them, hotter than even in their teenaged years.

Together, they fight to keep Bree alive and discover the culprit behind the attacks. In the process, they unearth a clue about the disappearance of the Iron Horse patriarch.

Preorder Soldier's Duty Now!

ABOUT THE AUTHOR

ELLE JAMES also writing as MYLA JACKSON is a *New York Times* and *USA Today* Bestselling author of books including cowboys, intrigues and paranormal adventures that keep her readers on the edges of their seats. When she's not at her computer, she's traveling, snow skiing, boating, or riding her ATV, dreaming up new stories. Learn more about Elle James at www.ellejames.com

Website | Facebook | Twitter | GoodReads | Newsletter | BookBub | Amazon

Or visit her alter ego Myla Jackson at
mylajackson.com
Website | Facebook | Twitter | Newsletter

Follow Me!
www.ellejames.com
ellejames@ellejames.com

ALSO BY ELLE JAMES

Iron Horse Legacy Series

Soldier's Duty (#1)

Ranger's Baby (#2) TBD

Marine's Promise (#3) TBD

SEAL's Vow (#4) TBD

Brotherhood Protectors Series

Montana SEAL (#1)

Bride Protector SEAL (#2)

Montana D-Force (#3)

Cowboy D-Force (#4)

Montana Ranger (#5)

Montana Dog Soldier (#6)

Montana SEAL Daddy (#7)

Montana Ranger's Wedding Vow (#8)

Montana SEAL Undercover Daddy (#9)

Cape Cod SEAL Rescue (#10)

Montana SEAL Friendly Fire (#11)

Montana SEAL's Bride (#12)

Montana Rescue (Sleeper SEAL)

Hot SEAL Salty Dog (SEALs in Paradise)

Brotherhood Protectors Vol 1

Hellfire Series

Hellfire, Texas (#1)

Justice Burning (#2)

Smoldering Desire (#3)

Hellfire in High Heels (#4)

Playing With Fire (#5)

Up in Flames (#6)

Total Meltdown (#7)

Declan's Defenders

Marine Force Recon (#1)

Show of Force (#2)

Full Force (#3)

Driving Force (#4)

Mission: Six

One Intrepid SEAL

Two Dauntless Hearts

Three Courageous Words

Four Relentless Days

Five Ways to Surrender

Six Minutes to Midnight

Hearts & Heroes Series

Wyatt's War (#1)

Mack's Witness (#2)

Ronin's Return (#3)

Sam's Surrender (#4)

Take No Prisoners Series

SEAL's Honor (#1)

SEAL'S Desire (#2)

SEAL's Embrace (#3)

SEAL's Obsession (#4)

SEAL's Proposal (#5)

SEAL's Seduction (#6)

SEAL'S Defiance (#7)

SEAL's Deception (#8)

SEAL's Deliverance (#9)

SEAL's Ultimate Challenge (#10)

Texas Billionaire Club

Tarzan & Janine (#1)

Something To Talk About (#2)

Who's Your Daddy (#3)

Love & War (#4)

Ballistic Cowboy

Hot Combat (#1)

Made in the USA
Coppell, TX
22 December 2021